I0571690

What If...

Kelly Rae

WHAT IF...

© COPYRIGHT 2012 Kelly Rae
BLOSSOM PRESS 2012

ALL RIGHTS RESERVED

All rights reserved. Without limiting the rights under copyright reserved above, no part of this publication may be reproduced, stored in or introduced into a retrieval system, or transmitted, in any form, or by any means (electronic, mechanical, photocopying, recording, or otherwise) without the prior written permission of both copyright owner and the above publisher of this book.

This is a work of fiction. Names, characters, places, brands, media, and incidents are either the product of the author's imagination or are used fictitiously.

This eBook is licensed for your personal enjoyment only. This eBook may not be re-sold or given away to other people. If you would like to share this book with another person, please purchase an additional copy for each person with whom you wish to share. If you're reading this book and did not purchase it, or it was not purchased for your use only, then you should return to your online retailer and purchase your own copy. Thank you for respecting the author's work.

Dedication

Of all the things I have ever done, or will do, being a mother is by far my most treasured. I take more pride in my son's successes, than my own. Triton, you once told me that I was like MLK's mom, because she believed that he could do anything, and I tell you the same thing. I was beyond flattered for the comparison, but the truth is that you make me believe that I can do anything. Your love, confidence in me, and your sacrifices are what made this dream of mine, a reality. Next stop (besides Cali)…making all of your dreams come true!

To the moon, and the stars, and all the way back, you are always my Best Guy, I love you!

Acknowledgements

I have been fortunate in my life to have the love and support of many. Perhaps this is the true measurement of success. To look around and see people who love you, support you, and lift you up at every opportunity; this has been true of my life, and I am blessed.

Thank you to my parents, all four of you have shaped me, loved me, and supported my dreams. Mom and Bonnie, thank you for the safe haven you offered me to write this book, you are truly one in a million!

To my little sister, Rachael, whom I adore and whom I find I not only love, but also enjoy more and more all the time. I treasure you!

To my older sister, April, I have such deep gratitude for you. That you are a lover of books, a teacher of life lessons, and my touchstone. I am so blessed. Moreover, you gave me precious nephews, Orion and Gabriel, Auntie loves you!

Angelica, I will be forever thankful that you showed up in my life right when I needed a soul mate, I love you most! Kids for your support, your love, and confidence in me I thank you. We make a great family; I love you all day, every day!

Tammy and Vena, there is no one with whom I would rather cast a spell. Through the years and all the changes, I couldn't have done it without you. Tammy my most fervent cheerleader, I still want to be just like you when I grow up!

To my Jensen, for understanding and making me laugh through it all, ("Don't make me come down there ..."), I love ya!

To finish this book, I moved to a small town in Central Oregon for some peace, quiet and well...cheap living. In this town, I found a lot more than I bargained for, so to the Bronze Beach Bombers your friendship is invaluable.

Shantel, I am honored to know you; the friendship and friends you have brought into my life have made this town an amazing stop along my adventure.

To my family, by blood and by choice, I love and cherish your tireless encouragement, loving embrace whether I am near or far, and the knowledge that you are always waiting and ready to welcome me home!

Prologue

*K*atie sat on the dilapidated porch of a girl she barely knew, waiting for her dad to arrive. The area was lit by a single bulb, with no fixture, eerily humming next to the front door. Katie's house was homey and clean. This house was run down and depressing. Katie hadn't been impressed, upon arrival, with the vitamin green house or its front yard of brown grass and dead foliage. Now, with pieces of the wooden deck digging into the back of her legs, she was even less so. She had only worn this skirt because it was a warm spring night and it felt good to finally feel a little warmth in the air. She hadn't planned to need protection from splinters.

Luckily, she had at least thought to bring a light sweater for when the cool night air arrived. The garment was now doubling as Kleenex. It was all she had at her disposal and it was better than the alternative. Her mom would have been furious if she knew Katie was using her sleeve to wipe the snot from her upper lip, but there was no way in heck she was going back into that house with tears flowing down her face and a snot mustache. It was the best she could do as she sat and patiently waited.

The party she was attending had been her boyfriend Chris' idea. He was rapidly becoming more popular now that he had gotten involved in sports and was excelling. Suddenly people, who had not noticed either of them, were paying close attention. Katie was honest enough with herself to admit that Chris' popularity had surpassed her own and she was now his plus one, rather than he being hers.

She didn't mind so much, she had seen the fickle side of popularity before and she could deal with being the supporting player as long as Chris didn't treat her that way.

Now out of his shell, he was funny and much more charming by the day. He was the star and she was happy for him, mostly. They had gotten into a few fights recently about his new attitude, because to her it seemed he was letting the attention get the best of him. Katie didn't like the big ego he was toting around town disguised as his head. She was the reason he had tried out for sports in the first place, she was the one who had helped him with his GPA to be eligible, so she had hoped he would be more appreciative, or at least treat her as well as he had before he got popular. Clearly, that was not going to happen, because here she was on this porch, weeping and oozing visible signs of sadness from her entire face.

Katie vaguely heard sirens off in the distance, but didn't give them too much thought. She was busy trying to calm herself, trying to control her breathing with deep, long breaths of air. Unfortunately, every time she breathed in all she could smell was jasmine. She never understood why everyone loved jasmine so much. It made her nose burn, eyes water, and well, it stunk. So, at the very least she could tell people it was a bad reaction to jasmine that had her eyes swollen and leaking.

The sirens were closer; she could hear them even through her own sobs, snot, and sorrow. Her dad would be there any minute and he would make her feel better. He always did. Scraped knees, hurt feelings, bad grades, he had a way of making them all seem better. When Katie had called him to come and get her, she could tell that he was worried. He kept asking her what was wrong, but she couldn't get the words out past the tears. She could barely get out the request for a ride home.

The emergency vehicles seemed ever louder or maybe there were just more of them, it was hard to tell. Katie was worried her dad might be delayed if traffic was blocked; for what sounded like a big accident. She thought she could pick out an ambulance siren now and maybe a fire truck, it was impossible to discern the different sounds as they mixed together in a sad melody. Behind her, the music was still loud and the voices of her peers laughing and gossiping about each other started to fade away. The pit of her stomach began to ache. Dad wasn't here yet, it had been at least ten minutes, maybe more, and they didn't live that far away. Katie heard the front door open and looked back to see Chris standing there with a concerned look on his face.

"Katie, what are you doing out here? I've been looking all over the house for you." He had the nerve to sound perturbed. He stepped closer to where she was sitting and she put her hand up to tell him to stop, before she stood up to face him.

"Really? All over the house, huh? Too bad I wasn't in that brunette's mouth, 'cause then you would have found me right away." She snapped at him.

Immediate guilt washed over his far too handsome face. His eyes, the most amazing hazel, often said more than his words. When he was sad, they were glassy, as if he were stifling tears. When he was happy, they seemed to be smiling just as much as his mouth. And when he was being a joker or mischievous, which was ninety percent of the time, they sparkled like the night sky. He couldn't hide much if you paid attention to his eyes.

"What are you talking about?"

"I'm talking about walking into the basement looking for you, since I thought we were at this party together, and finding you with your tongue down some other girl's throat! That's what I am talking about, Chris, and if you try to deny it, I'll just scream. I am so mad at you right now."

Katie was in his face now and he flinched at her words. She had not physically touched him, but his body reacted as such. He furrowed his brow to offer an indignant expression and then as if he decided on a different approach his brow went limp, he took a breath, and his voice went soft when he spoke.

"Princess, you don't understand. It wasn't my idea, there was… a bet and well, I lost, and it totally wasn't a big deal. No tongue and it was just because I got dared. Seriously, it was nothing."

Katie had stopped listening at 'Princess, you don't understand' because she knew the rest would be a lame excuse. Plus, she thought she could hear the sirens getting closer. Her dad still wasn't there. What was taking so long?

"Katie, are you listening to me?" Chris demanded with a stomp of his feet, like a child.

"Chris, I don't believe you, I know what I saw. Don't treat me like a fool I'm… "

Just then a mixed color of lights were projected onto the house and Katie turned to see a sheriff's car pulling into the driveway, headlights on with red and white lights flashing but no sound. When the deputy got out of the car, her knees gave out and she just about hit the deck. He was here for her, she could feel it down deep in the pit of her stomach.

Chris had been right behind her and caught Katie before she fell to the ground. Katie was screaming stop, go away, in her head but nothing was coming out of her mouth. She closed her eyes, willing the scene to be different when she opened them again. She felt like a small child hiding from the boogieman, if she couldn't see the deputy then he couldn't see her, right? She would open her eyes to find him gone in five, four, three, two…

"Katie, are you ok?" Chris was yelling at her, for how long she couldn't be sure. She opened her eyes and there was the deputy, almost right in front of her now. Her mouth wasn't working; her throat felt dry and closed up, swollen like a bad sore throat but with no pain. Numb.

The deputy, who was now standing on the walkway at the front of the house, was Deputy Talbot; he went to her family's church. He had three kids, all younger than Katie, and they were always a little wild during the sermons. He was soft spoken and pleasant at church, a man with an easy smile her mom always said. His wife on the other hand was loud, even her whispers were loud, and Katie listened to them every week. She was constantly shushing the kids or trying to keep them from climbing all over her or the person next to them in the pew. Now he was standing in front of Katie and Chris, while Chris still held her upright. Deputy Talbot looked tired or weary maybe, she wasn't sure which. However, there was no smile for her tonight.

Deputy Sheriff Talbot did not have a good news face on. She didn't want to look at his eyes, because they looked sympathetic and she didn't want to be someone who needed sympathy. She checked out his uniform instead, a safe place to look. His hat was a little crooked, sitting on top of what she knew was drab brown hair with spatters of grey at the temples. His dark blue uniform pants were a tad too short.

Katie wondered why he didn't do something about that, it sort of made him look silly, less official. His shirt, although a little snug over a beer belly figure, was nicely pressed. She wondered if maybe his wife ironed them, just so, each week. That would be a nice wife thing to do. Her mom would have done that for her dad if he had been a cop. His hand reached out to touch hers and she noticed he had very hairy knuckles, but they were soft and gentle.

"Katie, I need you to come with me. There has been an accident." Deputy Talbot stated.

"What kind of accident?" She heard Chris asking from behind her. Deputy Talbot never took his gaze away from Katie; she could feel it on her as she studied his boots. Black. Scuffed. Tightly laced. Deputy Talbot didn't acknowledge Chris' question.

"Katie, I just need you to come with me please, your mom is on the way to the hospital, and I need to take you there to be with her."

"It's my dad, isn't it? All those sirens, those were for my dad."

"Yes, I'm sorry sweetie, your dad was in an accident and I need to get you to your mom, okay?"

The way he phrased it sounded like a question, as if she had a choice. For a moment she thought what, if I say no... will it make this all go away? Deputy Talbot grasped her other hand and started to nudge her forward, helping her to walk. Her feet were lead. Her head ached from all the crying and the effort it took to simply exist. Her mouth was so dry, it tasted foul and felt stuffed with cotton. She knew she needed to try to walk, to make her feet move, but there was a serious disconnect between her brain and her body. Chris didn't seem to want to let go, she felt him tug her back when she tried to move. Then, when he did release her, he let go very slowly, but she pulled away from him and let Deputy Talbot take her right arm and guide her to his car. She was almost to the vehicle when she stopped.

"What happened?" She queried.

"I am not sure of all the details, I was called to the scene at the end to assist with traffic control, but I do know someone hit your dad's car and they are all headed to the hospital now." Katie's head snapped up to look at Deputy Talbot.

"Was my mom with him?" Her heart stopped waiting for the response.

"No, another deputy was sent to get your mom when I left to get you. Your dad was lucid for a few moments at the scene and he insisted that someone come here and get you, so I came right here. He said you were waiting for him and would be worried. I promised him I would get you. But that's all I know. We need to get you to the hospital right away."

It was just like Katie's dad to make sure he took care of her even before he was taken to the hospital to receive care for himself. He was always thinking of her first, his Peanut; he had never let her down. Tonight was no exception. Her thoughts were interrupted by Chris' voice still right behind her.

"Katie, do you want me to go with you or follow you there?" She couldn't see him; the lights from the car were so much closer and blinding. In truth, she didn't want to see him, in this moment, anyway. Her dad was on the road because of her, to rescue her from a broken heart. Chris... he did this. Chris tried to touch her arm, but she pulled away immediately. He was the last person she wanted touching her. He came around to try to force his face into her view.

13

"Katie look at me please, are you okay? Can I go with you, please? I want to be there for you and your mom. Please, at least look at me." Chris tried to touch her chin and nudge her face up, but Katie jerked away and continued walking with the deputy. "Katie …"

She didn't respond. She didn't have the words to express how she felt even if she had wanted to talk to him. She just wanted to leave and get to her parents. She wanted to be there for her dad, so he would know she was okay and safe. Make sure he used his energy for himself and not worrying about her. Moreover, she needed to be there for her mom. Dad was the strong one he always took care of things. Mom was fragile. Katie needed to be the strength for her that he usually was, until he got better.

Deputy Talbot sat Katie in the front seat of his car and when she looked out the window, there were now a bunch of people out on the porch. They must have seen the lights flashing, but she didn't remember hearing voices or even the front door opening. At the very front was Chris, who looked somewhere between shocked and like he was about to cry. They probably couldn't see her with the lights flashing, but she had a good view of them. Like spotlights overhead, they shined light on the crowd. Next to Chris was *the brunette*. Katie didn't know her name, or even recognize her, so she probably didn't go to their high school. She was a little taller than Katie was, thin, and pretty. She too was wearing a skirt, although a much shorter one than Katie. The brown-haired person must not get cold, Katie thought in a snarky moment, because the shirt she was wearing was more like a handkerchief than a blouse.

There he was standing on the porch with half of their high school class and the troublesome girl hanging onto his arm, she was comforting him she supposed. Katie was at a loss for words. He looked like he was talking but she decided it didn't much matter what he was saying or to whom. She looked at him and in that moment, while Deputy Talbot was buckling up and putting the squad car in reverse, she didn't feel any of the usual emotions associated with Chris. Usually he made her feel loved, giddy, and warm, usually he made her feel special. She would have preferred to feel nothing rather than the burning, evil feeling that was taking over her heart.

"I hate you" she spoke, but it came out like a whisper more than words. Chris' face changed, as if he had read her lips, which she knew was impossible with the lights. He started to walk away from the porch and down the driveway toward the vehicle. He raised his hand, almost in a wave goodbye or maybe to ask her to stop, but Katie simply put her head down to cry. Everything changed that night. Katie didn't recall much after her arrival at the hospital. The details seemed unimportant in this case, the end result was all that mattered.

She never saw the first man she ever loved alive after that night, and after his funeral, she made a point to never see the first boy she ever loved again either...

Chapter One

...Ten Years Later...

*N*o rest for the wicked they say, although Katie couldn't recall ever actually being particularly wicked. She would like to think that she would remember such an activity since she rarely even got close to mischievous. Nonetheless, work was insane, and she was in the thick of it all. To tell the truth, she felt great getting the chance to jump right in and start taking on some cases of her own. The crimes around Pennsville and the rest of the county were not exactly up to Boston standards.

A little over a decade of life outside this small town, she had returned to take the job of a lifetime. At least she was hoping it would turn out that way. She had been at her new job in, her old town, for about two months now. As Assistant DA, she got the first look at most of the smaller cases to see if they seemed worthy for Paul, her superior, to consider. So far, there had been a few small town cases brought in for consideration, but nothing worth pursuing by the DA just yet. Most of the cases in this town never even made it before a judge.

After the first month Paul even let her write many of the witness questions and recently a few closing statements. He said she had a flair for the dramatic without making it seem like a Hollywood production. Katie was beginning to think that moving back to her hometown had been a positive change, and despite her hesitation when she first arrived, remaining in Pennsville was a real possibility.

It was Wednesday night and Katie was getting ready to leave her office, which after two months was finally set up to her liking, when the phone rang.

"Katie Wright's office, may I help you?" she wanted to sound like a receptionist in case she did not feel like speaking with whoever was on the other end.

"Hey, Kates, it's Sarah. I forgot when I invited you over tonight that it was my little brother's first basketball game of the season. Do you think you might want to come with us and maybe get a pizza afterwards?"

"Well..." Katie hesitated and was about to say no when Sarah interrupted,

"Actually, you know what, you don't get a choice. Meet us at the high school and we will save you a seat. I'm sure you remember how to get there. We'll be on the home side. The kids are so excited to see Darren play. See you there, honey. Bye."

Sarah must have known Katie was going to bail on the idea, so instead she gave her no choice. Katie could call her back, but chances were she wouldn't answer. Over the last few weeks, she had spent as much time with Sarah as they could both fit into their schedules. Katie worked a lot, and Sarah had work and a family to juggle, but both seemed to find time. It had taken Katie weeks to contact Sarah, mostly because she was afraid that Sarah would be mad about the way Katie and her mother had just up and left Pennsville her senior year of high school. No goodbye and no looking back. Nevertheless, Sarah was sweet and kind, and had welcomed Katie home with open arms.

Katie could not remember the last time she had a real friend, someone with whom to share laughs and the day-to-day concerns that make up a life. Sarah had reminded her how much she missed having someone in her life that cared for her, that wanted to know about her days and be there for her no matter the circumstances. Well, other than her mother of course, but she lived hours away. Katie felt like it was changing her, like maybe there were a few walls she had built that were a little weaker than before. Since Sarah would be there, Katie wanted to take a little leap and face up to her fears a bit. She could handle going to the old high school, she had to face it all eventually, and tonight seemed like as good a time as any. She had Sarah for support and she was an adult. Not to mention that it had been a decade since she sat in the stands and cheered for her home team and Chris.

Katie never really thought about it these days, but she had been fairly popular in high school. She never had a problem finding dates and she was just pretty enough for girls to want to be friends with her and not so pretty they hated her. Katie remembered it being treacherous for some girls in school. She guessed, overall, high school itself was not the worst experience of her life. She should get over the fear and go watch a silly basketball game. With renewed confidence, Katie got her things together and left her office to head out to her car and back to high school.

Why it is that in one moment years can disappear, and any sense of who you are slips away when you recognize a face or the sound of a voice? Even a song played on the radio can transport you back in time. As Katie drove through downtown Pennsville Station, her mind took her back to when complexion breakouts were a huge deal, and boys still made her nervous. What a simple life that had been. Of course, at the time, it had all seemed highly important and complicated. Katie remembered herself as a teenage girl, and was struck by those same fears and feelings.

Katie hadn't been back here in almost eleven years. Leaving Boston and the big city where you could get lost in a sea of people to return to this small town where everyone knew everyone and all their business was a big change.

The car seemed to slow all on its own as she rolled into the downtown area. It looked the same, and yet somehow Katie felt so different. Growing up, she assumed, did that to a person and a hometown. The buildings all looked the same, although not all of the businesses remained. One thing that made her smile was to see *Martha's Ice Cream Haven* still in business. The zebra-striped awning hanging from the front, slightly faded from the sun, made her feel nostalgic. She could not even begin to count the amount of ice cream she had consumed in that shop. She pulled over and opened her windows hoping she would be able to smell the fresh waffle cones, made fresh by Martha all day, every day. Katie smiled as the scent wafted by. Her first real date had ended with a shared sundae at *The Haven,* as locals referred to it.

The butterflies in her stomach had been relieved a little by the sweet taste of mint chip ice cream and chocolate sauce. The flower boutique where she got her first corsage was still there, although it had a new name. *Violet Val's* was now painted on the awning of cream and purple in black lettering. Main Street used to have only stop signs; today she went through two stoplights and could see another coming up on her way to the high school.

Leaving here, her senior year of school had been difficult, but Katie and her mom hadn't been able to handle the memories after they buried her dad. A drunk driver hit Sam, her dad, while he was on his way to pick Katie up from a party. That night she lost more than just her father. She lost her first love, Chris, as well. Not because he had died in the car accident, but because it had been Chris' fault. His fault her dad was on the road, his fault that she called her dad crying and asked for a ride home. Returning to this town forced her to think of so many things she had avoided for years. This town triggered thoughts of Chris and all she lost at a very young age. Tonight wasn't about Chris, it was about having fun and letting go of old business. Her life here before was old news and she wanted to start over, start fresh with a new life and people.

Katie parked her car and took a quick check of her appearance in the rear view mirror. Her lipstick, a deep wine color, was still present. She glanced up and did a quick check on her mascara and eye shadow, which was a conservative shade of brown, offset with a soft pink just above her lash line. The color combo always made her blue eyes pop, with a little help from her black mascara. She was a little over dressed for a basketball game in a black two-button suit jacket paired with a knee length skirt and heels. She was used to a conservative dress style for the office, due to her time in Boston, she even wore panty hose. A bit much for the occasion, but she wasn't in the habit of having a change of clothes handy at her office, so this would just have to do. Her father used to tell her, that it never hurt to be the best-dressed man in the room and that was why when casual Fridays started he still wore a suit to work. Hopefully, his theory applied to this situation as well.

Katie walked into the gymnasium, catching sight of Sarah and her family right away. The gym looked the same, a new coat of paint being the only noticeable difference. The bleachers were brown, wooden, and about twenty-five rows deep when pulled out from the wall. The floor had a big orange T in the middle, for the school's mascot, the Tiger. Katie made her way across the side of the court and over to the home side of the gymnasium. She had been a regular here in high school, two games a week each basketball season of her junior and senior year. There was probably an imprint of her backside along one of the lower rows. Katie made her way up, closer to the middle of the bleachers, to find a spot with Sarah.

Sarah's mother and father were there as well as her other brother, the middle kid, Steve. Katie had not seen Sarah's family since she had been back, and Steve had changed dramatically. Last time she saw him, he was a geeky 13-year-old boy with braces. Now he stood before her, arms stretched for a hug, a 23-year-old man with a face that must melt the hearts of every girl he met. He had a dimple on his chin that begged her to reach out and make sure that it was real. He was at least a foot taller than he had been when she left town. If his girlfriend had not been sitting right next to him, Katie might have taken the time to check out the rest of him. He was beyond young for her and he was her friend's little brother, but he sure was a cutie.

Everyone was trying to catch up on one another's life when music started to play over the PA system signaling the boys' entrance to play ball. Katie was sitting between Sarah and her Mom, and she was not as nervous as she thought she would be.

"Where's Tom?" Katie asked when she sat down 'I thought this was a family thing and I would get to see the most amazing husband ever." Sarah looked upset and simply said,

"He had to work late so you will have to wait for another time to see Mr. Wonderful." Katie could tell Sarah was not happy with Tom, based on her tone. Katie went to say something, but Sarah shook her head in what Katie took as a request not to push the matter, so she let it drop. It would be something they would get back to at some point, but not in front of her family.

While the boys were warming up, Sarah's mother, Erica, asked Katie about her mother.

"Dear, I hope you don't mind me asking, but how is your mother these days?"

"She is doing well, thank you. She moved to Montana years ago and lives on a ten-acre piece of an old ranch." Katie hoped it did not sound as isolated and lonely as it was.

"That's nice, dear. All by herself?" Erica questioned.

"She has two horses and a few other farm animals to keep her busy." Katie replied. "It's really been a nice change for her, but we miss each other."

"Do you think she might ever come here for a visit?" she asked.

It would be nice to have her here, but Katie did not think it would ever happen. Rather than admit that, Katie responded,

"She just might someday, when I am all settled in here."

"That would be so nice, dear. It would be lovely to see her again."

Katie let the conversation die down and concentrated on the court instead as an excuse to look away.

The game was already underway; Katie had missed the first few shots. She looked around studying all the championship banners covering the walls. There were many more than when she was a student. Apparently, the basketball team had been very good in the last four, or five years, because there were several regional and state champion banners hoisted above the shiny wood floor. Katie mentioned it to Sarah, and she said,

"We found ourselves a new guy, he is a good coach." Sarah said with a smile that Katie could not decode.

"Oh, well, that's great. I'm so excited to see Darren, and it's been so long since I was here. Wow, it brings back so many memories, huh?" Sarah looked at her and just shrugged her shoulders. "The truth is," Katie whispered to Sarah, almost embarrassed to say the words aloud, "I was scared to come here. For some reason I could not get it out of my head that I would see people from the old days. Luckily, they are not old enough yet to have high school kids. Looks like I am in the clear and I can relax and just enjoy the game. Thanks again for making me come, Sarah." Sarah started to say something and then just said,

"It really is the best thing for you Katie, and I honestly believe that."

That was a little dramatic, Katie thought, something was definitely up with Sarah.

Katie had to admit she had not been watching much of the game due to her roaming eye, but she started to notice that they were winning, and that Darren was great. He was making shots and handing off for assists like a mad man. She still remembered a few things she learned about basketball from sitting and watching Chris play in high school. She was a faithful fan, back then. The other team took a time out, and for the first time she looked at the bench. There were two coaches.

One coach looked familiar. Katie thought he might be the same person who coached when she was there, so he could not be the great find. Then she noticed the extremely lanky man sitting next to him looking down at a white board. He was busy yelling out instructions to the kids, gesturing wildly, while the old guy nodded. Mr. Lanky was clearly the one in charge of the team, despite not being the head coach. How refreshing, most people could not handle the ego bruise of not getting the full credit for a job well done. The time out was about to expire, and the team huddled together. The younger coach stood up and as he walked toward the kids, her breath caught. She could not believe her eyes. No one had mentioned to her that he was back in town, he must have moved back too or else why would he be coaching the team? Katie quickly pinched Sarah under the arm to get her attention.

"Ow-ah, what's the matter?" she had the nerve to say, in a too loud voice. The group around them turned to stare a bit at them. Katie did the "mom whisper" that her mom used to do when she was a kid. With a clenched mouth in a fake smile and closed teeth, she whispered.

"You know exactly what the matter is, and don't try to play innocent with me. Why didn't you tell me he lived here? Why didn't you tell me I was going to be forced to see him tonight? I can't breathe, oh my God." Katie's heart was racing, her breath was labored, she was pretty sure that her feet were no longer attached to her, they were so numb.

"I wasn't one hundred percent sure what you knew, we haven't talked about any of that yet. We have both been avoiding the big, tall, handsome elephant in the room. We talked about your dad and your mom, but never Chris. I was waiting for you to bring it up, I guess. I didn't tell you he would be here, because I didn't want you to run," Sarah said.

Katie still could not breathe. She was looking at Sarah but not really seeing her and she heard her speaking, but barely caught the words

"Katie, I know you don't socialize much, so I figured there was no one else that you work with or speak with who knows it might matter to you that Chris Staller came back here to live. I know you are happy here now, so I figured it would be okay to let the cat out of the bag. Besides it's fun to see old friends, right?"

Katie was not 100% positive, but she thought she heard Sarah saying this was fun. How could she be so callous? She had just finished telling her that she did not want to see anyone from the old days. She meant random friends and acquaintances – but this was Chris Staller. He was the last person she wanted to see ever, anywhere, and here he was and Sarah thought it was fun! She needed to breathe, so she took a deep breath and then another. Sarah was lucky that Katie did not want to be noticed, because every cell in her body wanted to scream and pummel Sarah, friend or not.

"If we weren't in a public place, I would be kicking your ass right now, Sarah." She was taking deep breaths, trying not to draw too much attention to herself. Breathe in, breathe out, deep breaths was the mantra she repeated in her head to remain calm.

"Calm down," Sarah said, with an almost irritated tone. "It's not that big of a deal. He probably won't even see you, he is a little busy you know. Relax and enjoy the game. Think of it this way; you have the upper hand, because you know about him and he may not know about you."

How could this be happening to her? It was bad enough she had to face the family demons here, but now there was this. Chris Staller, here in Pennsville. The last time Katie had seen his face he was on TV, during a party at her college dorm to watch College Football.

When Katie saw his face on ESPN, her first instinct had been to smile. Smile, that he made it to college, that he was successful enough to be talked about on ESPN, and because he looked good! The sportscaster mentioned that he was receiving an award for having the highest GPA for his school's athletic department. Her college roommate was watching as well and could not believe Katie knew him. To brag a little, since everyone teased Katie about being a hermit, Katie mentioned he was her high school boyfriend. Sally, her roommate, was shocked and told her what a hottie he was. She referred to him as sweaty, which apparently had been a good thing, although Katie never understood why. When her roommate asked what happened Katie just said it was a long story, and it had not ended well. Sally was always a little more sympathetic towards her about dating, after that day. She could use a little sympathy now. She could not believe how seeing him affected her. She just hoped Sarah was right, and he did not spot her.

She made it all the way to half time and then tried to leave, but Sarah and the family would not think of it and insisted she stay, especially since she had yet to say hello to Darren. Katie knew that meant waiting for him to get out of the locker room when the game was over. That left a lot of chance for contact with Chris, but it seemed really important to them. The truth was that she was not sure she could make it down the bleachers. She had stopped hyperventilating, at least.

She could not get up but at the same time, leaving was the only thing she wanted to do.

Her legs simply would not cooperate. She felt frozen, glued to the bleachers. The teams came out of the locker rooms and warmed up a bit before the second half. Katie could not take her eyes away from Chris on the sidelines. He looked good, she was hoping that up close he would have wrinkles and a receding hairline and any number of other imperfections. At the same time, she did not want to get close enough to know for sure. She decided she needed to get out and quick.

"Sarah, I just can't stay, this is too much. Please tell Darren I am sorry and that I will stop by to see him very soon. Tell him I am sick or anything you want, but I just cannot do this tonight. I'm sorry."

Sarah did not get a chance to reply; Katie just stood up and started to shimmy across the aisle of the bleachers to try to get out. Why did people move so slow the faster you wanted them to go, especially when you were in a hurry? Katie was almost to the end when she looked up to see Darren huddled up with Chris. She watched as Darren pointed into the stands, and they both looked towards Sarah and family. She felt like a deer in headlights, frozen and unable to blink. Chris waved at Sarah, and she thought maybe there was still a small, minute, minuscule chance she would get away with this; and then he saw her.

For a moment, his smile grew and without her permission, she smiled back. Her heart swelled and beat a little faster. Quickly she got control of her face and forced the smile away. Then his smile faded and her heart deflated at the sour look left on his gorgeous face. He must have been just as shocked to see her, as she was him. The buzzer sounded to signal the start of the second half of the game. The trance was broken.

She found her feet and was able to get herself down the bleachers and into the restroom. A quick wash of her hands, a little cool water on the back of her neck and a good look at herself in the mirror was in order. Katie had always gotten herself in trouble repeatedly over one small human emotion. Pride.

Katie looked at her own reflection and all she saw was a coward. Who cared if he was here, so what if he saw her, and so what that he did not hold a smile and run over to her? So what? Why that thought even popped in her head she was not sure, but at some level Katie was a little upset that he did not seem more excited to see her, damn him. She was the one who had a right to be upset, not him. She looked into the mirror and gave herself a good stare-down.

"Katie Wright, don't you dare be a wuss. You don't back down from anything and you sure as hell aren't backing down from this." The woman looking back at her this time was determined, she reapplied her lipstick and strolled her little behind back into that gym and shimmied her way back into the seat next to Sarah.

"I thought you were leaving?" Sarah said to Katie with a smirk on her face. Katie's only reply was the look of death. God help Sarah, for the rest of the night and maybe longer as she was on Katie's shit list. This was about pride and nothing else; no one got the best of her, especially not Chris Staller.

The rest of the game she tried not to look in his direction at all. Every once in a while she thought she could feel his eyes on her, but maybe not. For all she knew, he could care less that she was here again, for all she knew he wished she had just stayed away. She was afraid to look at him, afraid to make eye contact, so she just kept her eye on the game. It was a great game, and Darren and his team did an excellent job. They won sixty-six to fifty-four. It was fun to watch these kids enjoy life and play a little. Adults always seemed to lose that, and even as a kid, Katie did not have a lot of that playfulness. She waited with Sarah and the gang until Darren came out of the locker room. Everyone congratulated him, and when he got to her, he gave her a hug.

"I'm so happy to see you." Darren blushed.

He had been seven the last time she saw him, so it was nice to know he even remembered her. Katie had not spent much time making friends in recent years, she had forgotten how nice it was to have people care for you.

"I can't believe you remember me at all. You were just a little thing last time I saw you. Now, you're all manly." His whole face turned red.

"How could he forget the first girl he ever loved?" Steve said in a crappy, big brother way, which made Darren so red he was practically purple.

To relieve his embarrassment, Katie pinched Steve under his arm and over his utterance of pain assured Darren, "Well, a girl never forgets the first guy to share his Oreos with her, either."

So far, that made two family members pinched in one night. She was not sure what was going on with her and the pinching. One thing she did know was that her window to sneak out before seeing Chris up close and personal was closing quickly. As she was making her get away, she saw him out of the corner of her eye, and without thought turned to see him better. He just about took her breath away, close up as he was now. He was taller than she remembered, and lord, did he look gorgeous. He wore a dark blue suit with a black shirt and coordinating tie. Time had been kinder to him than to most of the men she had seen around town and knew from high school.

His face was tanned and had more character than it did at 18, but the laugh lines only seemed to enhance his face. His shoulders were full and so very broad. Since all of her memories of him were as a boy, it was startling to see this man standing before her. He still had a spark of playfulness in his eyes.

Katie watched him as he smiled at someone across the room, and there it was, that same boyish grin on his now grownup face. Oh my, he was H.O.T! It was just about the worst possible thing he could be and wasn't it just her luck that he did not turn out bald and 80 pounds overweight. Damn it! He was absolutely magnificent, and she had to force herself to look away.

"Sarah, I have to go," Katie whispered, "I can't talk to him and try to act normal. I just can't do it." She did not wait for a response this time and just took off. Katie tried to look nonchalant as she got the hell out of there. Dignity made her walk slowly, so as to seem confident and in control. When she got to her car, she quickly started the engine, blasted her music, and took off with a little screech of her tires. As she looked in her rearview mirror, she could swear there was a tall figure standing outside the gym watching her leave.

That night as she lay in bed, she found herself fantasizing about when she and Chris knew each other better than anyone in the world. How strange that she could not even bring herself to speak with him. She dreamt that night of innocent kisses and first love, and when she woke for just a split second, she felt warm and loved. There was an easy joy and a feeling of safety. It was a sense that she had not known for a very long time. It was as if she still lived in a world where her daddy would always be there to save her, and she was sure that her Mr. Wonderful was just around the corner. As soon as she was ready, he would be there to whisk her off to his castle, his heart belonging only to her.

Waking up some days was a harsh reality. This morning the difference she felt when she first awoke made her think. Where was the line between being an independent woman; capable of taking care of herself without any need of a man in her life, and just being plain lonely and desperately wanting a man whether she needed one or not? She was starting to think she was more the latter than she had realized. Seeing Chris had stirred something in her and she did not like it, not one bit.

Admittedly, she had control issues. She realized that it was next to impossible to expect that she would never run into Chris, now that she knew they lived in the same town. It was out of her control. However, the way she reacted to him was completely in her power. As she got herself ready for work that morning, she made a promise to herself. Chris would never know that he affected her in anyway. She would treat him like any other person she used to know in town. She would treat him like who he was, "just" an old high school boyfriend, and nothing more. She put her power suit on and fired up her power mind set. After all, how hard could it be?

Chapter Two

*I*n the weeks following that game, Katie had been busy enough with work, but still could not forget that night. She had seen Sarah since and made up with her, although she was aware that one more of those surprise attacks and she could say goodbye to Katie's trust and quite possibly their friendship. Sarah explained that she was just trying to help her, but all she really did was magnify the pain Katie had tried to bury. Just talking about Chris clearly made her uncomfortable, and though Sarah did not bring him up often, it was not something that could be avoided entirely. Sarah mentioned him one afternoon when they were having coffee.

"So, Chris asked Darren how long you have been in town and tried to find out how long you'll be staying. Darren told him that you live here now, and then Darren asked Chris if he still had the hots for you – his word, not mine." Katie was not sure what to think of this conversation.

"Well, I guess it would make sense for him to be curious about me. I am sure it was a shock for him to see me, just as it was for me to see him. Thank you again for that, my dear friend."

"You really need to let that go." Sarah snickered, "It needed to happen. It's not like you would have been less shocked had you seen him anywhere else and hey, at least this way there was a crowd for you to hide in."

"I love how you still insist it was a good deed, you brat. It's over and done with, so, as you said, let's just drop it. It has been almost 3 weeks and I have yet to run into him. If I do, I will be polite and that's about it. I mean, I'm sure he told Darren he did not "still have the hots" for me and was just polite about it." Katie stated, although it came out sounding a lot like a question she realized.

"He told Darren it was not appropriate to talk about women being hot with his students."

"Oh." Katie sighed, sounding more disappointed than she meant to. Sarah just chuckled and Katie gave her the look, which Sarah was getting with alarming frequency lately.

"You still haven't really explained why you are so against catching up with him, I mean for heaven's sake, the man has seen you naked. If memory serves, I believe he was the first to do so, what's with all the attitude?"

"It's complicated." Katie sighed and decided it was time to confide in Sarah. "He was with me the night of the accident. He is sort of mixed in with all of that in my head." Katie got quiet for a moment and Sarah just let her be, "You know that my dad was on the road to come and get me from a party. I don't even remember the name of the girl hosting the party anymore, but I guess it's not important in the grand scheme. I called, he came to get me, and he was hit. He would never have been on the road without that call. I feel… well, I called, so I feel at fault." Katie's eyes watered up and she felt a tear roll down her cheek and then another.

When Sarah reached out to touch her hand, she used the other one to wipe the tears from her face. She despised crying, especially in front of people. And now she was sitting outside what was supposed to be a trendy French café with metal tables and the most horribly uncomfortable metal bistro chairs in the world, crying. Even the napkins were rough, so there was no solace to be found in them either.

"Katie, sweetie, it was an accident. You cannot accept the blame for a single bit of it. You needed a ride home and that is what parents do. You didn't do anything wrong. It was just an accident. The only blame lies with a drunk who also paid with his life and that of his daughter's. His fault, not yours! Your dad was simply doing what he would always do and life just sometimes takes people away before we are ready for them to go. That is certainly not within your control."

"Oh, Sarah, it doesn't feel that way." Katie grimaced with pain as she said the words, "I was mad at Chris, I saw him kiss another girl and I was crushed. So I called home for a ride."

"Oh," Sarah uttered, "'So that is where Chris is involved - you never told me *any* of this."

"I didn't talk to anyone before mom and I left. I was ashamed. I still am. Sarah, I was crying so hard when I called my Dad, I know I scared him. I couldn't even tell him what was wrong. Just that I needed a ride. My heart felt broken when I called home, but I had no idea what a broken heart was until later than night at the hospital with my mother."

"I love you Katie, but sometimes you are too hard on yourself... and everyone else around you too."

The two friends sat for a long time in silence, Sarah's hand on Katie's, sipping coffee and watching people as they came in and out of the café and milled around the downtown shops.

"I don't know about you Kates, but these metal chairs are about the most uncomfortable thing I've ever sat in, so before I have squares permanently etched into my backside, let's get out of here."

Katie nodded her agreement and they left. In the parking lot, Sarah gave Katie a hug filled with more emotion and sorrow that Katie had let out in a long time.

"Thank you for sharing with me. I know it's hard for you to do. I am always here, call me anytime you need to, okay?"

Katie nodded her agreement.

"And I want you to promise me you'll think about what I said. You need to release the blame; you cannot own someone else's responsibilities. For the record, I don't mean blame Chris. He was a kid, same as you. The *adult* drunk driver, he owns this, not you. Please promise you'll really give that some serious consideration."

"I promise." She replied half-heartedly. "I'll think about what you said."

That night, lying in bed, Katie thought about her conversation with Sarah and for the first time in a long time, considered the idea that maybe the accident was not her burden to bear, not completely anyway. She would have to think on it some more, but the reality was that without that phone call, her Dad would have stayed safely in bed. If she had not been so upset that night, if Chris had been a better boyfriend, he never would have kissed that girl. He would have given her a ride home that night and her father would be alive. Chris seemed to remain the center of so many emotions and thoughts these days.

At first, Katie had been concerned that Chris would try to seek her out, but it had been a few weeks with no contact, so she figured she was safe. If she were honest with herself, she would admit that she was a little disappointed. But, when it came to Chris, she was simply still too messed up in the head. No contact. It was for the best and it made it easier to believe this move would pan out just fine.

In the meantime, her professional life was center stage. Paul was throwing more and more work her way, impressed with her quick grasp of how the team operated. Every county and office was a little different. Paul was not kidding when he told her she would be spending more hours at the office than in any home she rented. He joked that she should invest in a cot. If the coffee had been better at the office, she might have considered it.

As it was, she had to stop every morning on her way in at the fancy new Cup-O-Java stand she found. She ordered the biggest cup they had each morning, knowing she wouldn't be able to get a second cup at the office. She only ventured in to the break room for a mid-cup warm up. All jokes about break rooms are based on reality and this one was no exception. The fridge smelled like two-week-old lettuce and cucumbers and no one seemed to want to clean the counters or the microwave regularly.

On Katie's first week she had cleaned the thing twice, but had since given up on it like everyone else. Amazingly, it was always the same three people in the break room, sitting at the standard wood veneer table in the crappy chairs all break rooms have. No matter what time of day she ventured in there, Larry, Curly, and Mo were there. She got the impression that they excelled in all day, every day breaks excluding Saturdays of course. She knew this because she was a Saturday "regular". She was the only one crazy enough to work weekends, as though the small town office were no different than bustling Boston.

During regular business hours she spent most of her time with Paul, and eventually, he suggested that

Katie meet his wife. Or rather, his wife suggested she get to meet Katie.

"My wife thinks she needs to meet you, so she can decide if she's okay for me to be working late into the night with you. I made the mistake of telling her that you are one of the brightest assistants I've seen in a while. Oh, and I may have also mentioned that all the men here at the office are crazy for you."

Paul was a few inches taller than Katie's five foot nine inches, in her two-inch work heels. She was not sure of his exact age, but she placed him somewhere in his late forties to early fifties. Paul had dark brown hair with gentle streaks of silver-gray here and there. It was just enough to look distinguished, wise. His eyes were the palest blue, almost like the sky, and so very kind. He had been an amazing mentor so far and Katie felt blessed to be under his tutelage. She felt honored that he wanted her to meet his wife.

"I'm happy to meet her, Paul." Katie said. "Anytime. It would be an honor. However, you really shouldn't exaggerate my appeal around here. The men don't even look at me."

"Katie, it's truly amazing that you don't know how beautiful you are. It actually makes you that much more irresistible. The real exaggeration is my wife thinking a sweet, beautiful girl half my age and far smarter would be interested in an illicit affair with me. That's the real lie here."

They both laughed at that one. Paul was much more of a father figure to her than anything else. He had taken her under his wing, and that was that. He was a wonderful man, but for her to be interested in him he would have to be tall and broad, with dimples and a great chin and... Damn, there was Chris again. Why was he continuing to pop into her thoughts? She could not keep from thinking about him. He may be drop dead gorgeous and, according to the grapevine, he was one hell of a coach and role model for the kids, but he was still the same Chris Staller that she had permanently cut off in high school, and that made him off limits.

"How am I going to get him out of my head?" She said aloud. Luckily, Paul was used to her mumbling and did not even notice she was talking. How are you going to get his image out of your mind, Katie? How?" She asked silently this time.

She was supposed to meet Paul's wife at a dinner party they were hosting Friday night. Originally, it was to be a small party with just the three of them and a few others from the office. Then the day before, Paul informed her that the party had gotten bigger, and now the group of five or six became a crowd of twelve to fifteen. Katie was not thrilled to say the least. The last thing she needed was a dinner party with people she did not know, who wanted to ask a bunch of questions.

People she met in town were always intrigued by her story. They wanted to know why she left, which was not as easy to explain as why she came back. She didn't like talking about the accident and yet so much of her life stemmed from her reaction to that night. It made meeting new people uncomfortable at times. Paul told her not to worry, that he and his wife would help keep the topics off her and try to be a good buffer. She and Paul had never spoken about her past in Pennsville, but he knew what had happened because he had been working in the DA's office when it all went down. The only mention he ever made was to tell her he was sorry about what happened. She trusted him not to make it a difficult night for her, but as it turned out, she should have made the pact with his wife.

When Katie got to their house she was immediately impressed, especially since Paul's desk at work resembled a crash site. Either he took more pride in his home than he did his desk, or his wife took care of things around the house. The house was much bigger than it appeared to be, from the outside. It was an older home on a large, but narrow lot. The house was lean and long, including a proportionately long dining room and a proportionately long, but elegant table fit for a queen. There were sixteen lavishly upholstered chairs set around the largest table Katie had ever seen, also lavishly set for dinner. The house was decorated in shades of wine, a merlot couch with bordeaux pillows, drapes in a "subtle" hue of cabernet. Katie only knew this because naming each color had been a highlighted part of the tour, which had amused her to no end.

It was unusual, but dark. The narrow shape of the lot restricted the positioning of the house, leaving very little in the way of an east-west exposure to sunlight. This was compensated for with a rich and warm décor. The only light colors in the house were the walls, which to Katie's surprise were not just light, but stark white. Between the antique style furnishings and the deep colors of the décor, Katie felt like she had stepped into a small modern day castle. It fit Paul's wife perfectly.

When Paul talked about her, she came across as a bit domineering, but he seemed to love her a great deal. Smitten was the word that came to mind. Her name was Helene, and although she was not exactly what Katie expected physically, she fit with Paul well in spirit. She was more delicate in appearance than he made her sound in personality. She was petite, with small linear features and seemed almost too physically delicate for a man like Paul. Katie was the first to arrive, as planned, so that she could meet Helene before the rest of the crowd got there.

"Oh, my," Helene said when Katie had walked through the door, "I don't know about all these late nights, Paul. She is even more enchanting than you described. What am I going to do?"

Katie couldn't tell if she was kidding or not by her tone, but the look on her face was more jovial than genuinely concerned, so Katie assumed she was trying to be amusing.

"You are being far too kind," Katie said. "But it's lovely to meet you. And please, no more worries about late nights at the office. As far as I'm concerned, and I think Paul will hate to hear it, he's more like a father figure to me than anything else."

"See, honey," Paul said extra loud, "She thinks I'm a father figure, so I doubt she wants to jump my bones."

"Oh, Paul, don't speak like that. Besides, if there's any bone jumping around here, they will be mine."

Katie could not help but smile at them, and although she felt awkward at first, she quickly settled in, figuring out that this type of banter was normal for them and had little or nothing to do with her presence.

Within twenty minutes, the doorbell started to ring and the first few guests trickled in. People from work were the first to arrive and she was glad, because she felt comfortable around them. Most of the other guests she recognized from her childhood. Some of them had been friends of her parents. They seemed to be looking at her as if waiting for her to say something, but, other than a pleasant greeting as introductions were made, she remained quietly reserved. Everyone seemed to be waiting for Katie to make the first move and admit she recognized him or her. They'd have a long wait, she was not particularly outgoing in a new crowd, let alone her "old" crowd. In what she felt was a polite span of time; she excused herself to the kitchen.

Katie was helping Helene in the kitchen when the doorbell rang.

"Oh, good," Helene whispered at the sound of the doorbell, "that must be Coach Underman. I can't stand his wife, but when he's around, she's bearable."

Katie smiled at Helene and continued to help fill the serving dishes with the food Helene had prepared. Between the size and appearance of the dining room and the food Katie was dishing, it was clear that Helene went all out for a dinner party. She had prepared roast lamb with a mint garnish, baby potatoes, caramelized carrots, gravy from the meat drippings, and a green salad with croutons, cranberries, broccoli pieces, her own balsamic dressing, and homemade rolls. It all smelled delicious and it took great willpower on Katie's part not to sample a bit of everything.

Katie was carrying a large dish of potatoes to the dining table when she looked around the room of guests and saw Chris standing in the living room. She was fairly certain that she actually gasped, but was not one hundred percent sure it had been audible. She looked for Paul, and he must have seen the distress written on her face, but all he could do was shrug his shoulders.

In the office, when someone on the staff would exasperate either one of them, they would shrug their shoulders as if to say "I can't believe it either" but Katie did not think the shoulder shrug applied to this situation at all. She gave him the closest thing she had in her arsenal to the evil eye. What could he do but look at her as if he was sorry. Katie knew it had to be a surprise to Paul as well. Chris was not looking in her direction, so it gave Katie time to check him out a bit. He seemed so very tall this close.

He was wearing a silvery blue sweater under a navy sports coat and dark slacks. He looked casual, but appropriate for the dinner party. She noticed that he did in fact have a little bit of a widow's peak happening, but it was early stages. She could not detect any other defects to speak of, but surely, he must have a couple by now. If only there were some physical flaw she could latch onto, it would help immensely. For the moment, she just needed to stop staring at him before he noticed her.

Katie managed to keep the potatoes in the bowl and, with a bit of focused effort, place that bowl on the table. Then Helene called her name from the kitchen, and everyone in the living room looked in her direction. It seemed to her as if Chris moved in slow motion. She did not know what to do, when he turned and looked at her she simply held her head high, turned around and walked into the kitchen. She could not believe he was there.

Leaving was not an option, because the dinner was very important to Helene, which made it important to Paul, and that alone meant she was stuck. Of course there was also that damn pride issue she battled at every turn, especially when it came to this man. Why had she gone and promised herself that she would never let him know he affected her – what kind of lame idea was that? Hindsight is so very 20/20. When Katie stepped into the kitchen, she questioned Helene as politely as possible.

"Helene, did you invite Chris Staller to this dinner?" She was trying not to seem too upset about the whole thing. She was already thinking that if Paul had known all along, he was going to hate working with her for the next few weeks.

"Oh, yes, honey. It was sort of a late invite, because I knew he would be at the gym with Coach and I thought it would be nice to have at least one person here your own age."

This meant that, as furious as Katie was - and she was livid - Helene had made an innocent mistake, and as much as she would love to wring her neck, Katie controlled her anger. It would certainly not look any better on her to be all flustered when she walked back into the dining room. In the moment before Katie was going to respond to Helene, Paul walked into the kitchen and immediately started to apologize.

"Katie, I am so sorry I didn't know he was invited. Helene, why is Chris Staller here?"

"I was just telling Katie, because I thought it would be nice for her to have someone her own age at the dinner party, and I knew Coach would be running late from practice, so it just made sense to invite Chris. Why are you both making a federal case about this?" Obviously, Helene was out of the loop.

"Honey, do you remember me telling you how Katie was having a hard time adjusting to living back here again and that she saw her old boyfriend and it through her for a loop? Remember honey, I told you *where* she saw him, and *what* he was doing?" Helene looked confused and then the light went on.

"Oh my, I have messed things up this time, haven't I? You said it was at the basketball game, and he was a coach, but I completely forgot that whole conversation until right now, and I feel like an imbecile. What are we going to do now?"

"What we are not going to do," Katie said with great bravado, "is panic and act like anything is wrong. We are going to finish getting the food on the table, and then we are going to have everyone sit down for dinner and eat this wonderful feast. I don't want either of you to act frazzled, because I refuse to seem upset about this."

She was pointing at them, as if she was scolding children, the whole time feeling that her face was beet red. Katie was the one who needed to calm down. "Okay, you guys go out first, and I'll bring the last plate out in two seconds. I just need to compose myself and then I'll be in, just please make sure I do not have to sit next to Chris." Helene and Paul moved quickly. They both looked afraid.

It was almost comical, she thought, how quickly they moved out of the kitchen. She felt like a drill instructor. It took her a moment to feel the flush start to leave her face, and then she quickly picked up the gravy boat and walked into the dining room. Her heart sank when she noticed everyone was seated, and the only spot left was directly across from Chris. Fantastic. Obviously, she did not make herself clear enough. Sitting directly across from him was not only no better than sitting next him, it was worse. They would now be looking directly at each other throughout the entire meal. Katie did not have any choice but to sit and get this dinner underway. What a wonderful evening this was going to be...

Dinner felt strained for conversation at first, in part because Katie was the topic of conversation and that was the last thing she wanted to entertain. Everyone had questions about law school, Boston, and of course, why she chose to move back. While she really didn't need this kind of attention, it did allow her to focus on something other than Chris. She was almost sure that the warmth she was feeling was the heat from his body. On a couple of occasions when she allowed her eyes to innocently wander in his direction Chris' eyes would lock onto her, but each time Katie instantly averted her eyes from him.

The heat of feeling him watch her seemed strangely comforting. Maybe familiar was a better word than comforting. Comforting implied ease and she was anything but at ease. Throughout the meal, Katie could not bring herself to say a single word directly to him. By the time everyone had finished eating, it was already eight o'clock and they adjourned to the living room for more chat. Katie kind of hid in the corner and let everyone else talk for a while. Eventually, the subject of the basketball team came up, and Chris was then forced to talk.

He had been quiet the whole night, but when he talked about the basketball team, he lit up and was very expressive. When he spoke of the kids and his job, he looked like a man fulfilled by his work. Then Mrs. Underman spoke up to the crowd.

"Now all we have to do is get him a woman to marry or even a girlfriend, and his life will be complete."

Katie couldn't help it, her gaze just went straight to Chris, and he turned away embarrassed. His cheeks were red, and when he looked back at her, for a moment it was as if they were the only two people in the room. She could not look away from him. His eyes were sad. She knew that look. Everyone else was watching him for a response, but he did not have one. He just kept staring at Katie, and she could not move

45

from his gaze. Finally, Coach Underman spared them both and spoke up.

"Leave the boy alone, Sally. He'll find the right woman someday and he doesn't need to be embarrassed in front of all these people."

With the sound of Coach's voice, Chris finally looked down at the cocoa mug in his hand, and Katie could finally look away.

"Don't worry, Coach," Chris spoke up, "I get enough of that from the kids at school. Someone always has a Mom or Aunt they want to fix me up with, so I'm used to being given a hard time about my love life."

When Helene brought out the desserts, Katie was relieved. Not only did they provide her with a distraction, but also now, she could leave soon and not seem rude. She was more than ready to get herself out of the situation altogether. Katie ate a small piece of cheesecake and sipped another cup of cocoa before whispering in Paul's ear.

"I'm going to head home for the evening." To which he whispered back

"I don't blame you one bit, I only wish I could escape that easily."

He proceeded to get up and help Katie with her coat in the foyer. She knew she had to say goodnight to everyone, so she went into the living room where the group had reassembled and announced her departure.

"Good night, it was a pleasure to meet you all."

"Oh, you're leaving so soon,' Mrs. Underman said, 'but you are the youngest one here. You can't possibly be worn out already." The group chuckled and Chris just stared, but Katie was not about to be persuaded or guilted into staying longer.

"True, true I am one of the youngest, but Paul here is a slave driver and he let me out early today for this party, but he will expect me back with my nose to the grind stone tomorrow. I really had a lovely time, and hope you all enjoy the rest of your evening." Sadly, after ten on a Thursday night was in fact close to her bedtime.

She was exhausted emotionally, and it manifested itself physically rather quickly. She had yawned every sixty seconds over the last half hour, or at least it felt like it. She thanked Helene and hugged Paul goodbye before leaving. The night was cold and she took a moment on the landing to adjust her coat collar and put on her gloves. Her car was at the bottom of the driveway and when she reached her hand out to unlock the door, she heard her name.

"Katie, please wait." Chris touched her shoulder, and she harshly pulled away. "Please, talk to me. It's unbelievable to me that you're home again and ever since I saw you at the game, I haven't been able to think of anything else. I just want to talk to you, for a few moments, please?"

"Chris, I can't. I'm sorry, but I just...ugh. Please just go back inside and leave me alone." With that, Katie got into her car and drove away. She could not help but look back, and when she did, was a little disappointed that he had listened to her and gone back inside. The first thing she did when she got home was call Sarah.

"Hello," a groggy Sarah said when she picked up the phone.

"I'm so sorry to call this late Sarah, but you'll never guess what happened to me tonight."

"Well, I'm awake now, please do go ahead and tell me." Having friends was a handy thing, Katie was discovering.

"Okay, so I went to Paul's for dinner tonight, well for a dinner party, and guess who was standing eight feet from me as I walked into the dining room with a dish of potatoes in my hands?" Katie knew it was probably not hard to figure, since very few things flustered her and Sarah knew it.

"Well, let me guess, since you are calling me at what has become the middle of the night for me, and you sound as though you are excited and on the verge of tears, all at the same time, it must have been Chris."

"Right you are my dear, and that is the reason I keep you around. Chris was there, he came with Coach Underman after they had a game, or practice, or some such thing tonight. I was shocked and I'm really hoping that he did not notice, do you think he noticed?"

"Were you talking five miles a minute like you are now?" she asked.

"Ha, ha."

Nevertheless, Katie took the hint and slowed down a bit to tell her what happened. How she left without letting him talk to her and how sad she thought he looked when she did. Katie admitted to Sarah that it was mean. She just could not stand there so close to him and chat like old times.

"Sarah, you know that I can do most anything I put my mind to and have always been able to, but with him it's different. I see him and there are so many emotions that pop up that I can't sort through them fast enough to select a response. At dinner, it was clear that he is very dedicated to those kids and apparently, he coaches several other sports on campus. He is also the Director of Physical Education at the high school and holds a seat on the education board. It was all news to me, since I didn't even know he still lived here until a few weeks ago."

"Katie, you seem to have forgotten that I did, or do rather, know he lives here and I know all this stuff. What you need to do is let me go back to bed now and we can talk about this tomorrow, after you have given some thought as to why a man you haven't seen since he was a teenage boy makes you a babbling, stuttering, nervous, and somewhat crazy woman after all these years. Especially since you haven't let the man say more than ten words to you, or said ten to him. So, you go do that and I will go back to bed now, deal?"

"Well, doesn't your sunshine wear off a bit when the moon comes out?" Katie said with a snorted giggle, "Sorry again about waking you up, since obviously you are no fun in the 'middle of the night'. Now you just go back to bed and don't worry, there is no need to talk about this again. I'm not crazy and this was such a non-event that I shouldn't have called you anyway. I think I am just amped on dessert. Please tell Tom I'm sorry, too."

"Lie to yourself if you want Kates, I do it all the time. Good night and sweet Chris Staller dreams." Without letting Katie respond, Sarah hung up the phone and left Katie to be buzzed on sugar and adrenaline all by her lonesome.

"Mphf, he doesn't make me crazy or nervous; I'm fine... perfectly fine!"

Chapter Three

*K*atie could not sleep at all that night. She ended up at work at six am, before she could stop in for a coffee. Even before the janitor, Mr. O'Malley, arrived for his morning rounds. By the time Paul arrived, Katie had completed half a day's work. He made a stop by her desk on his way for coffee.

"How long have you been here? There is a pile of stuff on my desk that was not there last night. Are you crazy? You can't keep these hours up forever. Besides, you'll make me look bad."

He smiled as he talked to her, but she knew that he could tell that she was not in a joking mood this morning.

"All right, what's wrong? Do I need to go home and yell at the wife for making your night miserable and causing you to lose sleep?" Katie did not respond, "Hello, will you say something, please?" She did not dare look at him while he talked. Katie kept her eyes focused on her desk in hopes that he would back off and drop the whole conversation, but he just went on and on for what seemed like ages.

"Well, if you'd quit yapping I might have something to say," Katie finally said and Paul smiled, "No, please do not yell at your wife. I'm sure she felt bad enough last night, and no I didn't get any sleep last night, and yes I promise I won't be here this early every morning. I might even leave a little early today and go look for some furniture for my house. If that is okay with you, boss?"

Katie faked a smile and tried to sound as upbeat as possible. It was hard not to let him see how tired and confused she was after last night. Damn that Sarah for putting ideas in her head, as if she wanted Chris or was attracted to him still. Please. No way! Katie was rethinking the "friends are handy" thought she'd had last night. Paul interrupted her inner argument.

"Of course it's okay. I think you deserve a few hours of mindless shopping. Take off whenever you feel the need, at least for today, that is. You can't actually leave for good though, okay?" At this point, she was willing to take time off from work, with no guilt on her part.

"Don't worry Paul, after seeing what this place was like without me, I couldn't possibly leave you high and dry. I'm also sorry for my attitude just now, I shouldn't speak to you so harshly. I'm sorry." She smiled at him with her famous smile. Paul tried to look offended before he accepted her apology, then he walked away to get his coffee, but she could see a little smile turning up at the corners of his mouth as he walked out of her office.

The rest of the day went smoothly. Katie finished the items on her to-do list for the day and after preparing her list for the next day, she left the building. It was before three in the afternoon, a first for her in a long time. It was quiet at the mall, which was about twenty miles outside of Pennsville. She looked at the sofas and considered buying a new bed for her guestroom, before she reminded herself that she had never had, and probably never would have, any guests. Certainly the old mattress her mother gave her for her first apartment after college would do for now. She ended up buying a new sofa, which would be delivered in six weeks, and a new dining room set, whereas before she was eating off trays from the couch. It was an expensive day, but she was not a habitual spender, so it was just a chunk from her more than adequate savings.

She went through the mall and checked out the clothing stores finding a few new items she thought would add to her work wardrobe and even a cute pair of shorts and a tank top that was all kinds of sassy. She wasn't sure when she would wear the new outfit, but clothes were a weakness, they always had been. Overall, it was the most relaxing afternoon she'd had since moving back. Work was great, but it was more than a full time commitment. She barely had time to take care of household chores, like making sure she had food.

Katie used her early afternoon to the fullest and stopped at the grocery store on her way home for some supplies. She often ate salads because they were quick to fix. Basically, anything that did not require a lot of waiting for things to boil or bake, were on her menu. She did not have the luxury of time most nights due to her work schedule. Besides, cooking for one was never that exciting, which was sad because she had a real joy for cooking when she did find the time and company.

While walking through the ice cream aisle deciding if she really needed the Java Chip gallon or not, she saw Chris and a blonde beauty turn down the aisle. The blonde-haired woman, who was pushing the cart, was about five-foot-two in tight, short shorts; a t-shirt; and, what Katie had to admit, were very cute Grecian sandals. Little Miss Thing was smiling up at Chris with obvious adoration. Oh, how she remembered that feeling.

Chris was sexy even in jeans, tennis shoes and a simple gray shirt. It looked as though he had come here straight from work because the shirt had what appeared to be the high school logo in the corner, right above his obviously firm chest. Katie was salivating, but then again, who didn't love a man with a gorgeous smile, firm chest, and what one could only assume would be an equally firm backside. Holy smokes, what was wrong with her? She needed to find another good-looking man in this town. This was just sad.

Chris was hard to not gawk at, but Katie finally forced her gaze back to checking out the ice cream in her hand instead of Chris. She knew he saw her and more than that, probably saw her stare just a second too long as well. She did not really know what to do with herself. It was not like her to feel this way. Men typically didn't have much effect on her, but for some reason, this one did. She quickly put the ice cream in her basket and moved out of the aisle. She did not look for him and luckily, the ice cream was her last selection, so she got in line and waited.

Then, to her dread, in the line just 2 feet to her left, she noticed that damn Chris Staller. He'd entered his line moments after her and was now standing right next to her. In her mind, his name was now officially changed to "That Damn Chris Staller". It fit how she felt about him more and more all the time. She could feel him glaring at her and sensed that he was hoping he could pull her to return his stare. She was just about to step up to pay for her items when she accidentally glanced in his direction. His eyes were right there when she looked up, and she could not possibly evade him then. To avoid feeling like an idiot she spoke to him first.

"Hello Chris, how are you?"

"I'm just fine, thank you, Katie." They stared at each other for a while and finally the petite blonde-haired woman next to him interrupted the staring contest by clearing her throat to get his attention.

"Oh, I'm sorry, Amanda. Katie, this is Amanda, my um… friend. Amanda, this is Katie Wright." For some reason when he said her name, it sounded sweeter than it really was.

"Hi Katie," Amanda said with a bit too much cheer for her liking. "Amanda, Amanda St. James. Aren't you the lady from the newspaper who moved here and is like the first female attorney ever or something?"

"Sort of, I'm the first female attorney to serve in the County's District Attorney's Office. There are plenty of other female attorney's." Katie never did have much patience for men or women with pretty faces and not much else. Pretty rocks, she called them. Amanda was probably a sweet girl, but she was no rocket scientist. Katie had the feeling she was barely out of high school. It was exactly what she would expect from Chris. She should not be disappointed, but she was.

"It was nice to see you Chris." Katie started to say her good-byes.

"Was it?" Chris said in a challenging tone, completely interrupting her.

"And it was lovely meeting you Amanda, have a nice evening." Katie said ignoring Chris' question. The store clerk was waiting on her, as were the people behind her, so it was only polite to end the conversation. In reality though, Katie was trying to spare herself the awkwardness of the situation.

Katie was paying for her items when she heard Amanda giggle a little, she looked over, and Chris was whispering something in Amanda's ear. He used to do that all the time to Katie. Sometimes the things he would say would be very inappropriate for anyone else to hear, other times it would be something silly. He was fun that way, goofy one minute and sexy as hell the next. He had always known how to make her smile.

As Katie walked out of the store, she saw Amanda standing at the end of the counter waiting for Chris to pay and Amanda said good-bye once again. Katie looked up to be polite and return the good-bye and found herself face to face with Chris again.

He was staring at her and she could barely get the word "good-bye" out before rushing to get out of the market. It was so hard to see him for so many reasons. It brought up all these old feelings, some of which were joy and love, and then it all turned sour and she could only remember the horrible ending. She wasn't sure she could ever look at him without thinking of all she had lost and the suffering her mother went through every day, being a widow. Maybe it was a bad idea being here, but at the same time, she really loved her job and wanted to stay. "I won't let myself run away from this town again," she reinforced to herself once she was alone in her car.

As she drove away, she saw them again and for a minute she thought Chris looked despondent, but how could he be when he had someone is his life who clearly seemed to be gaga over him? She called Sarah right away to ease her nerves from seeing him and especially from seeing him with someone else.

"Hello," Sarah said in answer to Katie's call.

"Hi, it's me. I saw Chris again and he was with a woman who is, oh, I don't know... don't know her enough to even comment on her. Nevertheless, I suddenly feel like a schoolgirl and I want to tell you every little thing that was wrong with her and how she

is so not good enough for him, but that would be silly,
right? Tell me that would be silly."

"Katie, honey, that would be silly. No matter who it
is, she won't ever be as good as you would be for him.
There is no reason to make comments anyway. It
would be beneath you to do so."

"I know you are right, of course, and it's not like I
want him anyway, it's just… oh, I don't know what it
is. But it stings a little that she is the one with him, not
me."

"Well, sweetie, whose fault is that?"

The next few weeks were routine. Katie found
herself at work more hours than not. She and Paul
were extremely busy on a child abuse case. A man who
lived very close to her old neighborhood was accused
of beating his son and, according to the victim, he was
beaten for defending someone whom his father had
tried to molest. Child abuse cases were her least
favorite; there was no way to get around the fact that,
sadly, no amount of "justice" could ever really
diminish the effects of the crime. Even when the guilty
were convicted, which was often hard to do, the victim
was still always a victim, and the scars were permanent.
This would be her first time to sit second chair in front
of the judge for this county. Katie was a little on the
nervous side and wanted to make sure that Paul was
completely prepared and that they both made a good
impression.

Most likely, she would do none of the speaking, but
it was important for the judge to see her face and
become familiar with her as a presence in the district.
Paul said it would help in the long run just to be seen

and for her to look busy and professional throughout the trial days. Katie was also being given a considerable role in all of the prep work.

One evening, only minutes after she'd arrived home, she got a call from Paul telling her that she was needed back at the office. He'd received a call from the sheriff's department; they had another juvenile reporting abuse by their defendant, Riley. The young man wanted to testify that he had also been molested by Riley. Katie hadn't even had time to change into her comfortable clothes, as she usually did upon arriving home each day. Instead, she grabbed her keys and purse, slammed her front door shut, and drove directly back to the County offices.

It was upsetting that there was another possible victim, but the reality was that the more accusers there were, the more likely they were to get a conviction. The more people to testify, the more believable the state's case would be. Still, to think of another child affected by the man accused, was horrible. Interviewing the victims in these cases always made Katie a little sick to her stomach.

When Katie arrived back at work, she went straight to Paul's office where she was quickly filled in.

"Riley is being accused of molesting another child, eight years ago, in the same home where he currently lives. A seventeen year-old boy told someone at the high school that he was afraid to go to the authorities, but he knew something about the man that was being accused of child molestation. According to our kid, he used to be friends with Riley's older son, Ron. Ron moved out this year at the age of seventeen and tried to get custody of his younger brother who is now eleven, but was denied due to his age and lack of income.

Anyway, our new witness frequently went over to play at the house in question. On more than one occasion, he said he spent the night and when he would be taking a shower Riley would enter the bathroom to brush his teeth or do something to "get ready for bed."

It was weird, but the boy did not think much of it for the most part. Then according to the statement the sheriff's department sent over, in one instance, Riley came into the bathroom and asked the 8-year-old boy to move over in the shower and he got in with him. It made the boy very uncomfortable and he asked to get out of the shower, but Riley refused to let him out, proceeded to fondle him, and forced the boy to fondle him as well.

According to the boy's statement, he was almost forced to perform oral copulation on our defendant, but the water went cold so Riley stopped. He warned the boy that if he ever told anyone, people would laugh at him, make fun of him, and that his mother would never be able to love him if she knew what they had done. When he recently found out there was another boy involved after all these years, he felt he needed to speak up."

Paul and Katie continued talking as they walked to his car. During the drive to the sheriff's station, Katie was silent, busily taking notes on the information Paul was relaying to her on their latest witness.

"Our new witness had confided in someone at the high school and that person called his parents. They all talked about it together before heading down to the sheriff's station. The school staffer is in with the kid now and the parents are waiting for him at home. Our kid, Joshua Stafford, has asked permission for the school administrator to be with him at all times and would prefer that his mother not hear any more than she has to about the details. The parents have agreed to this and my understanding is that they have signed an affidavit allowing the administrator to be in the room in their stead. At this point his parents only know the basics and Joshua wants to keep it that way."

Paul had started talking the minute Katie stepped into his office doorway and had not stopped until he'd completely covered the new information. They were now sitting in front of the sheriff's station. She could tell he was uncomfortable with the topic, as was any rational person regarding child molesters. Even people in prison had a distinct contempt for child molesters.

It was not the evening she had planned, but she felt even more strongly that they needed to get this man behind bars. It was obvious that his crimes were habitual; this was not Riley's first offense. The thought of anyone hurting innocent children sickened her.

"Thank you for calling me back in for this, you could have done this solo. I appreciate you letting me be a part of all aspects of the case. I am saying this now, because I may not be as grateful when we're done. I hate this part of the job, Paul."

"Me too, kid. Me too! Let's get in there and make it as painless for the boy as possible. I want to get Riley for this, and we can do it, Katie. I know we can win this one!" Paul plastered a small smile on his face and patted Katie's shoulder before he made the move to get out of the car and head into the sheriff's station.

Once inside, they were escorted to a waiting room, while a deputy was finishing up with the boy. Paul handed Katie the boy's school records. It looked as though he had been a problematic child until his freshman year in high school when his behavior remarkably changed and he became a decent student, including going out for and playing on several teams in the school sports programs. In junior high and elementary school, he was labeled as a troubled child who did not pay attention in class and needed extra care to meet minimum progression requirements year after year. It was noted that he was disruptive in class and needed to concentrate on learning more.

Later, teachers observed that he was unsociable, quiet, and pensive, though he got along well with the kids who tried to talk to him. Nothing out of the ordinary for some kids, but considering the turnaround... something must have changed.

He went from talkative, to the point of being disruptive, to quiet, and then to an active high school boy. He was now a junior, and his teachers' records reflected that he was witty, outgoing, and a decent to good student depending on the subject.

Paul tapped Katie on the shoulder and motioned that it was their turn to interview the boy. He was probably tired by now, as it was well into the evening, but they wanted to interview him while he was still willing to talk. When they stepped into the room, Katie was not a bit surprised to see Chris in the room with Joshua. Her heart skipped a beat at the sight of him, but that seemed to be the normal reaction these days. It made sense to her that Chris was someone this young man would turn to.

It was well known in town that Chris was a favorite among the kids and that they trusted him as a teacher, a coach, and a friend. It was evident that Joshua trusted him too, since he insisted that Chris stay with him throughout all questioning. The Stafford's must have trusted him as well, because they allowed him to be the adult present to supervise Joshua's interviews.

This was the first time Katie was in his presence and didn't feel like a nervous wreck, mostly because this was her turf and she felt powerful in that knowledge. Paul and Katie said hello and introduced themselves to Joshua, who instantly seemed nervous.

"Coach, I don't know that I want to talk anymore. It's been a long day and I'm hungry. Can we just go now?" Joshua looked tired and his eyes were red from crying.

"It's okay, Josh, I know you're tired, but I think this is the last of the questions for a while. Katie, I mean Ms. Wright here is an old friend of mine and there is not a kinder soul in the world. There is no need to be nervous. She's good people and easy to talk to. I'm sure someone can get you some food," Chris looked to Paul and Katie for their confirmation which they gave with quick nods, "and then I'm sure that the District Attorney's office won't keep you long."

Chris looked at her with eyes that pleaded to keep this short and agree with him for the boy's sake.

"Mr. Staller is right, Joshua, we won't keep you long, and I'll see about getting you some food right away. I'll bet you're thirsty too?" Joshua simply nodded and Paul stepped up and said he would get the food and asked her to start the questioning.

She had very little experience questioning minors, so this territory was a bit unfamiliar for her. In Boston, there was a separate division for minor-related matters and she'd rarely been involved in those matters. She started slowly by asking Joshua simple questions, like his age and what year he was in at school. She already knew the answers but they were non-confrontational questions that she hoped would make him feel more comfortable with her. When she asked him about the change he had gone through in his first year his answer overwhelmed her.

"Well, you see Miss Wright," he started.

"Please… call me Katie, I'd like you to think of me as a friend or at least an ally." She politely interrupted Joshua.

"Um, okay, well… after the incident with Riley, I changed. I never went to hang out with Ron anymore. That's the oldest Riley son; he and I were good friends in school. My Mom never really asked why, except she knew that I came home early that one night and told her Ron and I fought. I think she thought it was just one of those kid things that happens. Ron and I never really talked after that. I think he knew what his dad did and didn't know what to say to me anymore.

I'm not sure if he ever did it to Ron or if there were others before me, but it changed me for sure. I didn't have much to say anymore. And because I was so quiet in school, most everyone decided I was a nerd, but I wasn't really doing well in school. I couldn't concentrate and well, I was just drifting through each day. At home, it was the same thing. My mom asked me a few times right after if there was anything wrong, but I couldn't tell her and then she just got used to it I guess, used to a different me. I think I was just under everyone's radar.

But, when I got to high school, I met Coach Staller. He saw something no one else saw and he knew I was sad for some reason, I think. Maybe he just felt sorry for me, I'm not sure. He's everyone's favorite teacher at school. All the guys want to be like him and all the girls have a crush on him."

Joshua smiled a little then and looked at Chris who seemed a little embarrassed by the compliment. Then

Chris nodded his encouragement to keep Joshua comfortable in continuing.

"He talked to me every day in PE and soon he had me convinced that if I tried harder I could be good at the activities each day. That's why I tried harder in class and then he asked me to come in after school and start lifting weights with the football team. I never thought I would be good enough to play on the team, but Coach helped me out and taught me rules and plays, and I actually got pretty good. I actually had things to look forward to, something to think about that didn't knock me down all the time.

Then the coaches asked me to try out for the team. They had already started the season, but well, they said they were short on players. It was just the freshmen team of course, but it was a lot of fun and I learned a lot. My Dad works all the time and he has to travel a lot, so he's never really home and it was nice to have a guy to teach me stuff and be a guy with."

At this point Paul came in with a burger, fries, and sodas for everyone. Joshua took a few bites before he continued.

"Pretty soon, because of football, I had to be more careful with my grades so I paid more attention and I guess it paid off. My Mom was so happy to see me studying and my Dad even made it to a couple of football games. Anyway, then Coach convinced me to try more sports and now I play a sport each season. There is a chance I might even make the varsity baseball team this year, which would be awesome since I haven't been playing sports as long as some of the other guys. That's why things changed for me at school. You know, Coach told me that when he was in high school there was someone who gave him a chance and showed him he could be more than he ever thought possible, and it made me think maybe I could be like him too."

Katie looked up from her notepad and looked straight at Chris. Did he mean her? He must, there was no one else in his life at the time. She did not let herself focus on it too long, this was about Joshua.

"He said that's why he liked coaching so much, because he wanted to repay the gift he was given. That's what he gave me, the gift of knowing I could be better than I ever thought. Coach changed my life and made me brave enough to tell what happened to me after all these years.

I just hope that it doesn't have to get out too much, about what happened to me. I doubt people at school would understand."

Katie was still speechless and looking at Chris, who could not seem to look away from her either. The room was very quiet until Paul finally broke the silence.

"Joshua, there is no need to make the details public and since you are a minor we can make sure that even your name doesn't get mentioned. I can't promise someone won't find out it's you, but I can make sure the details are hidden. Uh, Katie, should we start the questioning now?"

Katie focused at the sound of her name. Rather than ask questions of Joshua, Katie simply said, "Joshua, please just tell me what happened and, I promise, you'll be on your way home soon."

Joshua told his tale and it matched the story Paul received from the original statement sent to him at the office. Joshua provided a bit more detail and Katie found it hard to hide her pain for him. She tried to keep her face from showing too much reaction, so as not to make the boy any more uncomfortable. It got a bit more graphic than the original synopsis that Paul had given her, but she had heard similar stories before. Joshua did very well and after a few questions from Paul and Katie, they thanked him for his courage, assured him that he was very helpful, and let the boy go home.

His father came to the room to see what was taking so long, and was relieved to see that Joshua actually seemed okay, had been fed, and could go home. It was almost half past nine and there was still school the next morning.

"Joshua, thank you so much for coming forward with this information, I promise you that there is nothing I want more than to see justice for you and any other victims of Riley. I'm sorry we kept you so late and thank you again. We may need to talk to you before the trial, but it won't be this bad, I promise." Katie spoke to him in a warm, almost motherly tone and held out her hand to shake Joshua's.

"No problem, Miss Wright. Please, just stop him. I don't want another little boy to be hurt like me." The look on his face just about broke her heart. Katie shook his hand and smiled at this young man who was braver than it seemed she could ever be.

Paul and Katie were stepping out of the questioning room when one of the detectives said she needed to speak with Paul right away. Paul asked Katie to wait for him and walked away with the detective.

"I thought you'd left," Katie heard Chris's voice from behind her and turned to face him.

"I rode with Paul and he needed to speak with someone briefly. Shouldn't you be going?" Katie still felt in control of her mouth and her surroundings and for once was able to speak coherently to him and make sense.

"I am." Chris replied, "I was just thanking a friend of mine on the force who was kind to Josh when I called to report that we had some information to share. It can be very intimidating to walk into these doors even as an adult, so it was important to me that Josh felt safe. He's a really good kid and I hope reliving this whole ordeal doesn't make him back slide." Katie could sense his dedication and affection for Josh.

"It seems like you've definitely found your calling. It suits you nicely and it's obvious you care very deeply for these kids. I'm happy for you, Chris… and, well, I'll just say goodnight. I should, uh, go see what's keeping Paul."

As Katie started to walk away, she felt Chris' hand on her arm, it was gentle, but she could sense some frustration in his grip.

"Are you ever going to give me a chance, Katie?"

He asked her with a tentative voice. It was as if he was afraid to ask the question or rather hear the answer. Just as Katie was about to answer, Paul called her name from down the hall.

"Katie, it looks like this is going to take a while. Can I get one of the guys here to give you a ride back to the office?" All too quickly, Chris spoke up and said,

"I can take her Paul, don't worry about it. Go back to work."

Paul looked at her for a sign to tell him what to do with that offer.

"Um, well I guess that will be fine Paul. I'll see you tomorrow and we'll go over the notes from tonight?"

Katie tried to force a smile, but found she was remarkably uncertain. All her "power" had been stripped of her the minute Chris asked if she would ever give him a chance. A chance for what? Katie thought. A chance to talk, a chance to be together again, there were many possibilities in that statement. Katie was still in shock over it and now she had to take a ride back to her office with him. She walked over to Paul and softly spoke into his ear.

"You are in so much trouble tomorrow, Mister."

Paul just smiled and whispered back.

"I know, tell me all about it tomorrow," then he raised his voice and his hand in salute to Chris, "Thanks Chris for seeing her back to the office safely."

With that, Paul went back to the detective's office and Katie started to walk to Chris' car. No surprise, he drove a very big black truck that was probably difficult for little people, like Amanda, to get into all the time. She could not remember when she had become so catty, but she could not seem to help herself.

"How *does* Amanda get into this truck? Poor thing, she's so short!" She was sorry she even brought her up, because her tone relayed her intention in asking about the attractive girl precisely.

"She manages just fine, actually. She only requires a boost every now and then." Katie was aware that he was mocking her, but did not care to get into a battle with him over his oh so petite, and more than just fine, girlfriend.

Chris started the truck and Katie sat as close to the passenger door as possible.

"Why is it that whenever I'm near you I get the distinct feeling you would rather be anywhere on earth than next to me? I don't think you could be any more snuggled to that door if you tried." Chris' voice was sharp and he was unmistakably upset.

"I don't know what you are talking about, if I remember correctly, you never were a great driver. I am just holding on to brace myself."

It was all that came to mind, childish yes, but easier than the truth. The truth was his smell was intoxicating and she wanted nothing more than to bury her nose in his neck and breathe him in. The truth was that her mouth was dry from being in this small space with him. Katie was hoping that if she could sit all the way against the door she would be able to fight the urge to touch him.

"Actually, Katie, I was a fabulous driver, I just couldn't keep my eyes or hands off you some nights. I doubt we will have that problem tonight." Chris's voice was raised a bit.

"Well, that would be a damn safe bet." Katie shouted at him. Katie was upset and could not pin point the reason, except that she was angry with herself for letting him get to her after all these years. Chris just made a noise in his throat and did not say a word until he got near the office.

"Katie, I wish you would talk to me without looking like you can't stand the sight of me. All I want is a chance to settle things and make it so that when I see you I feel happy, because I want to be able to smile when I see you… and then I remember, oh wait, she hates me – no smiling allowed. It's a shame that we can't talk to one another. It's a small town and well, I think we could be great friends."

They were now sitting in front of her office building and Katie did not know what to say. She couldn't agree to be friends, because she did not know if that was at all realistic.

"Chris," Katie said, "I don't know what to say except I can't be your friend right now, maybe sometime soon we can try to figure things out, but I'm not sure when that will be for me. I'm busy with work and that takes most of my time. What happened is complicated and it was a long time ago. Ten or eleven years changes people, and in many ways, I changed in a lot of not so good ways.

I can't give you the chance you are talking about right now, but maybe at some point that will change too. I just don't know, so please just let it go. I'll enjoy my new life here and you can go on enjoying yours. I'm sure Amanda is waiting for you, so I'm going to go to my office now. Thanks for the ride. Goodnight."

She had just stepped out of the truck when Chris spoke.

"Amanda and I broke up, so no, no one is waiting for me."

"Oh! Well, I'm sorry to hear that Chris."

"I should have broken it off for a long time, but didn't. She wasn't what I was looking for anyway. She was very understanding, I just told her that I wasn't able to give her what she deserves. I couldn't love her, because my heart hasn't been mine for a long time. I knew that the day my Princess showed up back in town."

His eyes were so intense and Katie could not bring herself to look away from them. It was one of the first things she had noticed about him all those years ago, his hazel eyes. They were more beautiful than she remembered and the way they used to shine when he looked at her, the way they changed colors with his mood, used to make her melt.

The school colors were green and black, so his Coaching Staff shirt in green brought out the nicest green tone in his eyes. There was a slight mist to the air and sprinkles began to fall on her face, shocking her back to reality.

"I better go inside," Katie said, "thanks again for the ride."

She closed the door to his truck and walked up the steps to enter the county offices. When she looked back, he was still there looking at her and Katie felt warm, and for the first time in a long time, a bit tingly. "Uh oh," Katie said aloud, "what is happening to me?" It scared the hell out of her whatever it was.

Chapter Four

*T*he State vs. Riley case took up her whole life for the next few weeks. There were other kids who came forward two weeks after Joshua and with them, there was more and more evidence supporting their case. Katie was delighted that it was going so well. She was working hard and more than once Paul congratulated her on the work she was producing. There were some hard-hitting questions to ask Riley and Katie found a way to plug almost every hole they thought the defense attorney might try to establish against the state. She was good and in this arena, she knew exactly what she was doing.

It was Friday and Paul insisted that she go home at five because she had been at work until seven most every night for two weeks. When she got home, she found a message from Sarah that they were having a BBQ the next day and were hoping she could make it. Everyone would be there, Sarah said, including her parents, and her mom was making all the desserts. Her mother's baking was Food Network quality, so Katie would be happy to taste test her confections all day. Mostly, Katie was happy to be spending her day off doing something fun and totally unrelated to work. She called Sarah but got the machine, probably because it was basketball game night, so Katie left a message accepting the invitation.

After a Chicken Caesar salad for dinner, a warm bubble bath, and a few pages of a book, Katie decided to get some sleep. It was her most relaxing night in weeks and she did not even think about Chris, well, at least not until her head hit the pillow. She could not seem to avoid him when she was alone at night, in bed with nothing to do but try and sleep.

Her mind rarely quit working and for the last couple of weeks she was having a hard time controlling her thoughts at night. She would dream of him in his truck looking at her saying he broke up with his girlfriend because she'd come back to town. What was she supposed to do with that? She couldn't just forget the past and say let's pick up where we left off, because then what? Did he think they would magically live happily ever after? If only it were that easy! She was actually starting to wish it were that easy, which might have been the reason for the dreams.

At about two in the morning, after being awake for almost an hour out of pure frustration, Katie shouted, "Chris Staller, why are you doing this to me?" No one answered of course, but it felt good to yell at him all the same. Sometimes her thoughts were far harsher than anything she would ever say to anyone, but she had no qualms in yelling them at her wall.

"I am attracted to him, yes, but that doesn't mean anything. It does not mean that we, I, should do anything about it; it does not mean I should jump his bones or anything. They are good looking bones and he's sure filled out very nicely in the last decade, but still, it won't work. I have been fine without anyone for a long time and I am fine now. I especially do not need him and all the baggage that comes along with him, so if he would just leave me alone and get out of my head, that would be good. Get out!" She yelled and then laughed at herself.

This place was making her crazy, period. She didn't know Chris was still living here when she moved, but now that she was here and work was going so well, the only option was to suck it up and deal. She could certainly handle living in the same town with him. No problem. With a renewed confidence, she closed her eyes and slowly drifted to sleep. However, Katie couldn't deny her desires in sleep; and if anyone had been in the room they probably would have heard her calling out to Chris.

Saturday turned out to be a beautiful day. Katie woke up early to do some chores before heading over to Sarah's for the BBQ. At about 10:30am there was a knock on her door, but when she opened it up, there was no one there. There was, however, a pile of purple roses at her feet. They were gorgeous and there must have been at least two-dozen of them. The only person Katie saw was a young boy of about 11 walking away from her house. There was a note attached, but all it said was:

If only they were as beautiful as you are, I'd keep them near me, since I can't have you – Charming.

Charming, huh. Katie had not forgotten that she used to call Chris her Prince Charming when they were in high school. He had been teasing her once when they first started dating about being a princess and she in turn had assured him he was NO Prince Charming. From then on, anytime he was annoying her, she would call him Charming. He laughed every time and he usually would stop whatever annoying thing he had been doing. It worked like a charm; he used to say to her back then. And he was definitely working the ploy now.

She was still thinking about it when Sarah called around eleven to make sure Katie was coming to the BBQ and asked if she would go with her to the store to pick out party wares. It was last minute, but sometimes with the kids everything was done last minute according to Sarah. By the time Sarah arrived, Katie was showered, dressed in her new shorts and tank top and ready to assist.

"Wow, you look gorgeous today." Sarah commented when Katie opened up the door.

"Thank you, I bought these a few weeks ago and this is my first chance to wear the outfit. I love the tank top. I know it's a bit sassy, but it's a nice day and when am I ever going to wear it if not to a BBQ?"

"No, it's perfect for today and it is nice and warm out to boot. Those are great flowers," Sarah pointed to the deep violet colored roses displayed in Katie's living room, "where did you buy them?"

She stepped inside so she could get closer and smell them. Their fragrance was sweetly intoxicating, Sarah expressed again how beautiful they were. Just as intoxicating as the man who sent them always seemed to be, Katie's mind randomly thought. Oh, bother!

"Actually, they were on my doorstep this morning with a note from a secret admirer. Kind of cute and a little creepy, you know? But no big deal."

"How boyishly charming whoever they're from. No idea, huh?" Sarah looked at her quizzically.

"Nope, no idea. Ready to go?" Katie did not want to hear her opinion on the flowers, because Sarah probably already assumed, correctly, that they were from Chris, and well, Katie just didn't want to talk about it or him. Oh, why was he doing this to her? Maybe he did not listen very well, but she thought she had made it clear that she preferred he stay away for now, maybe even for good.

"Yes, I'm ready," Sarah catching the hint that Katie did not want to talk about it anymore. They headed to the local shopping plaza for the party items.

"Why are you having this party, I don't remember you saying that there was an occasion?" She asked Sarah.

"Oh, no reason really. It's just a get together for family and friends. Darren had the idea, but I think he just wanted to invite his friends over to swim. He convinced me I should have a BBQ and then somewhere down the line he wound up asking if he could bring some friends. Teenage boys can be sneaky, huh?"

Katie laughed and agreed that Sarah had been suckered into a pool party for her little brother, but at least she had invited a few grown-ups so that it would be a fun party for her as well.

"Where's Tom? He hasn't been around much lately; he must be working a lot these days, huh?" Katie had noticed that Tom was almost never around and somehow, rather than being tactful, it came out rather abruptly.

"Well, don't sugar coat it for me or anything Kates. Now, I can't lie and pretend it's no big deal. I haven't really talked to anyone about this yet; truth is I haven't been letting myself think about it much. To answer your question, yes, Tom is working a lot, and yes, I am worried. I feel silly even saying it, but we have been married a long time, almost the ten-year mark. What if it's more than work?"

"Don't be ridiculous Sarah, have you asked him about it or told him that you are concerned? Since when are you shy about confronting the issues? You seem more than willing to confront mine," Katie said with a shitty smirk on her face, trying to make light of the situation.

"Because your problem I can fix, but my own, now that's a different story. Maybe, ignorance is bliss, in my case. Maybe, if I ask the question I'll get the wrong answer. I keep thinking that if I just ignore it, then it won't exist." Katie reached out and touched Sarah's hand.

"What are you afraid the answer is, honey?" Katie queried.

"That it's not work he is running to all the time," she looked over right into Katie's eyes and finished, "but a lover." she whispered. Katie squeezed Sarah's hand a little harder. What was there to say? She simply held Sarah's hand in silence until they got to the shopping center.

They went to two stores in the shopping center, picked up a few last minute snack items, and headed to Sarah's house. Katie asked to stop at her house, to pick up her car, but Sarah insisted that she would take her home later.

Katie never liked being anywhere without a car to get home, it was one of the residual issues from the past, but she figured it would be okay since it was just Sarah's house. When they arrived, Sarah's brothers were both there at the house, but this time Steve was there without his girlfriend. Apparently, breaking up was the thing to do around this town.

It did not take long for her to end up poolside playing volleyball with the kids and Sarah's parents. There were a few uncomfortable moments where she was almost sure that Steve was hitting on her. She was usually oblivious to the attention of men, but this was unmistakable, so Katie worked very hard at keeping her distance. And was very glad that she had kept her tank top on when she got into the pool.

It worked for the most part, until Steve and Katie ended up on the same team, where she missed the ball and lost them a point. It seemed twenty-three year-old men still found it amusing to dunk girls, in the water. Unexpectedly he jumped on her and they both went underwater. Not so cute, because when she finally got out of the water and out from under Steve she looked up to see Chris smiling at her. Perhaps it would be better described as smirking.

Oh, he was smug all right, then he winked at her, and she did not recall ever wanting to splash someone more in all her life. She could only imagine what he was thinking while he watched her wrestle with Steve, a kid compared to them in age. She could not seem to break the stare between them, but luckily, Darren finally saw Chris too.

"Hey Coach, I'm glad you made it to the party, help yourself to the food and stuff." Darren took off to chase Sarah around the table, because she was hiding the guacamole from him. He was known for eating it all himself and not leaving any for the guests, most of whom had yet to arrive.

Katie was getting out of the pool when Chris stepped over and handed her a towel.

"I didn't know you would be here today," he leaned in a little too close and she could feel his breath on her neck, soft as his whisper.

"Same here!" Was all Katie could think to say, and she did not wait for further conversation. Instead, she walked into the house, where she had seen Sarah headed, to hunt her down and scold her for setting her up. *Again!*

"Okay, Sarah, what's with the scheming? Why should I trust you or attend one of your functions if you are going to keep setting me up like this?"

"What are you talking about? I didn't set you up." Katie almost believed the innocent face and tone Sarah used.

"Why didn't you tell me that Chris was going to be here?" She demanded as she was pulling her shorts back on after drying off from the pool.

"Oh, is he here? Darren told me that he invited him, but that he wasn't going to be able to attend. So then, I thought the coast was clear to invite you, which is why you didn't get the invite until last night. I'm sorry, sweetie. But seriously, this in not Boston and you are going to see him at parties and stuff, so you might as well get used to it, right? Just think of this as practice and don't you even ask me to take you home early."

"What are you a mind reader?" Katie was just thinking that very thing.

"No, but I can see it in your eyes. You look defeated, and the Katie I know never lets anyone or anything get the best of her. I'm sure that you can handle spending a few hours with this man. Don't you let him, and the things that scare you, win."

Getting Katie to think it was a competition was the easiest way to get her to stay and face him. Obviously, Sarah was even more devious than she thought. Sarah knew that she was afraid to be with him, because of the way she felt about him. Which was confused, mostly.

How could she be so very attracted to a man she had hated for the last decade? Only the devil knows for sure.

"You are right, I can handle this. He is just a man, who used to be, a boy I dated. Why turn it into something else? I can treat him politely and just mingle with everyone else. See, I knew there was a reason I needed you when I came back to this town, even though you seem to be the reason I always end up running into him."

Sarah just looked at her and mouthed *whatever*!

"Okay, fine, I'm headed out to the back with the rolls. Do you need me to take anything else out there?"

"Nope, that's it, everything else I can get. Just go have fun. I'll be right out." Sarah uttered and went right back to finishing her food prep.

Feeling a little stronger and confident that she would not allow Chris make her feel uneasy, Katie stepped out onto the patio with a convincing grin and found a spot to soak in the sun. Steve came over and sat next to her with a smile. Katie returned the expression and hoped she could handle the young man's advances politely.

"So, what are you doing at a family party on a gorgeous Saturday?" Katie finally asked so they were not just sitting there smiling at one another.

"I wasn't going to come, until Sarah said you were going to be here. I don't get to see you that often, you know? So, are you seeing anyone these days?"

Katie was a little taken aback by his abrupt question, although she could plainly see by the expression on his face where he was going with this one.

"Little Stevie, if you have it in your head that you can dump your girlfriend, then go about asking me out on a date...well you can just forget it right now, Mister. For one thing, you are too young and another thing, you are like a little brother to me. Stop smiling at me like that." Katie remarked with a giggle she could not hold in.

"Okay, okay, but a guy has to try, you know?' He said with a shrug of his shoulders, "I had a crush on you for years and I thought this might finally be my chance. Of course, if you thought I was a little brother the whole time, then I was a little off the mark. Besides I didn't dump my girl just put her on the back burner for a while. You know, as a back-up for when you dumped me."

Katie could not help but laugh at his devious ways and he had a huge grin on his face, so she picked up a napkin and threw it at him.

"It's a good thing you are so cute or else you would get in a lot more trouble with women."

Katie was still laughing at his comment when Sarah called Steve in the house. He got up begrudgingly to help her in the kitchen.

Katie was still amused by the conversation when Chris made his way over to her sunny spot and the empty seat next to her. She ignored his arrival entirely, at first. There were a few more people there now and she had yet to make the rounds to introduce herself to everyone. She was more of a people watcher than a person who mingled in new groups. Katie could read people more accurately when she stepped away and watched them talk to others.

"Still like to sit back and watch people before jumping into a crowd, eh?" Chris asked.

"Some things never change I guess, even when it seems like everything has."

"I guess not," He muttered softly, "I hope you know you made Darren a hero today with all those boys. You should have seen them watching you pay so much attention to him. They were asking him who you were and if you were a college girl or not."

"Well, I certainly don't pass for a college girl in most circles, so I guess I should start hanging around sixteen and seventeen year-olds more often." Chris laughed and she even chuckled a bit with him. His was hearty, manlier than it used to be, God help her.

"Well, I never saw you in college, but if you looked that good in shorts and a tank top all the time then I imagine you had no trouble finding dates. You look gorgeous Katie, absolutely breathtaking. Even I envy Darren today."

"Chris, please don't start, we were having a decent conversation. Can't we just keep it light and polite, as if we were two people who just met at a friend's party? I'm willing to put everything aside for today, if you are. What do you say?"

"I guess we can do that for today, but eventually Katie you are going to have to talk to me. We can't keep ignoring whatever your issues are with me."

Chris did not look happy, but now all Katie cared about was that for right now, she did not have to talk to him about anything deeper than the weather.

"So, Katie, tell me about your work and how the hell you ended up back here after all these years?"

Katie spent the next half hour or so telling Chris all about school, being really young in her profession and giving it a shot in the big city. Chris listened intently and asked questions when appropriate and then he told her about his journey back to Pennsville. First, he shared about his life in college, then his injury, and eventually how he ended up back in Pennsville, because it felt like home to him.

"If I hadn't been injured who knows where I would have ended up, or what my life would look like now."

"You said you hurt your knee, but what happened exactly?"

"I was playing in a football game and my leg was broken badly, it wound up facing the wrong direction. That was bad enough, but the real problem was that my ACL was also torn in the process. Unfortunately, even when I had rehabbed the hell out of it and my leg healed, my knee just still didn't work well enough. I can play adequately for my job and some recreational stuff. I have to wear a knee brace some times and no pro football or basketball team would take a chance on me, at that point. If I thought I could do it I might have pushed it, but I knew better."

"Wow, that must have been devastating for you, I'm sorry Chris."

"You know I don't have any regrets anymore. For the first few years it hurt a lot and I was severely disappointed. Eventually though, I came to like my life, I love the kids and I am good at my job. Life on the road would have been fun too,' he smiled, 'and well, the money would have been nice too! What I have now is great, I figure this must be the place, the life, I was meant to have."

"That's a really enlightened way to see things. I know a lot of people who weren't making the grade, pun intended,' to which Chris chuckled, 'that took it hard when they had to drop out of law school and change course. Not everyone can chart a happy course after the disappointment. They can become bitter, you seem to have taken it exceptionally well"

"Oh I have, but you know I love this town. When I graduated it was the only place I wanted to live and life has been good. No reason to be bitter for me."

He seemed to be sincere and Katie was pleasantly surprised by his honesty and his attitude, even though it was not quite the same for her.

"Funny, I never looked back once I left. I didn't feel homesick or have any desire to come back." Katie offered.

"You didn't miss anything or anyone back here, huh?" The sadness was evident in his voice.

"Honestly Chris, no I didn't. It was rare that I let myself even think about this place. When I left, I left for good. I didn't want to remember this place. It was painful."

"Because of Sam?"

"Yes, because of my Dad."

"I'm sorry, Princess. I know how devastating it must have been for you to lose him. I was never as close to either of my parents, as you were to both of yours. I didn't really get the chance to tell you how it hurt me to see you in such pain. I wish I had the chance to do it over again, I would have pressed more. I would have made you let me in."

Katie was not sure how to respond, but she knew this was not the place to have the entire conversation and decided it was best to play it friendly.

"Chris, I didn't allow anyone to be there for me. It was a rough time. And now…well now I'm back here and every day it feels a little more like home."

"I am happy to hear that Katie, it's great to have you back, the place feels different, better, with you in it."

They moved on to other topics and managed to find a good, friendly, space while they sat and talked together. Katie did not miss Sarah and Darren smiling at them as they bustled around the party. Sarah had not planned for the party to be a ploy to get them together;

at least Katie did not think she did, but she surely was enjoying the show of it all.

Katie had two glasses of wine while sitting and talking with Chris about her work and then it was time for dinner. She was having a good time with all of the guests. She ended up talking to a very nice man that worked with Sarah's husband and although he was a bit of a close talker, he was kind and relatively interesting. He kept telling awful jokes, but Katie laughed anyway because they were so bad.

Dinner was delicious and everyone seemed to be having a great time. The conversation ranged from the weather to battle of the sexes issues, which was by far the most animated and lively of topics. Darren and his friends were hanging out, mostly in the pool, horsing around. Katie could not remember ever roughhousing in any pool at that age, to her the thought would have been silly.

For that reason, and because she was finally feeling the wine she had consumed go to her head, she got up from her patio chair and stripped off her shorts and tank top to reveal her itsy bitsy bikini and jumped into the pool. For once she did not even consider being shy. She tried to get to the gym at least three times a week and she thought it showed. She felt uninhibited, and it was so rare for her to feel that way. She just wanted to enjoy the moment.

When Katie came up from the bottom of the pool, several young men greeted her by asking if she wanted to join their volleyball game. She was a little surprised that they were starting another game, but why not, they were young and full of energy. She could handle another game.

"Of course I do," Katie said, "but only if I can be on Darren's team."

She spent the next hour playing with the teenagers. Soon almost every adult was in the pool, and they had a very competitive volleyball game going. Chris was one of the last people in the pool and she could not help but stare at him as he dove into the water. His body was mind-blowing and when he was all wet from the pool water, she kept visualizing what it would be like to touch his chest.

He had a little bit of hair on his torso, with a trail that went down his belly and she had the urge to follow the trail to wherever it may lead. She really wanted to run her tongue down his torso. Danger! Danger! It was more than she could handle, so she excused herself from the game, got out of the pool, and headed for the hot tub.

It was beyond warm, and it didn't help that she was already feeling a bit hot from her imagination. Sarah came into the hot tub with her and brought another glass of wine. Katie was not usually a big drinker but in an effort to keep her mouth busy, she sipped. All her lips and mouth really wanted to do were to touch Chris. Her body was basically turning on her. A revolt of her senses, her imagination, and her desires. She was silently damning her body. It occurred to her, rather rapidly, that it was not the best idea to drink more. She certainly did not need any assistance creating the naughty thoughts rolling around in her head.

"Sooo...you and Chris looked like you were pretty chummy earlier." Sarah stated with a smile.

"Don't get too excited. We were only making small talk. We have a truce for the day, so we talked about my work, college, then his work, and his college, that's about it, actually. You know a little 'Isn't it funny how we both ended up back in this podunk town?' kind of talk."

"Hey, this is my podunk town, and I am actually here by desire, not lack of choices, Missy." Sarah tried to sound hurt, but Katie knew better.

"Don't pretend you are upset with me. You know it's a small town with most of the stereotypes upheld. Whew, I think this wine and the heat are really getting to me now. This has been a fantastic day and the first really fun time I've had since, well...in a long time. Thank you." Katie was sincere with her words, it truly was the most fun she had had in years.

"I'm just glad you decided to come over and join the party. You can't spend all your time at the office or home alone, you know."

"I know," Katie replied, "And now I'm going to go sit in my favorite lounge chair, because I'm pretty sure that I'm drunk, and that hasn't happened to me since I was about twenty-two years old."

She got out to make her way to the lounge chair and was lucky to get there without falling. She stumbled the whole way there. The party was dying down and there was just the hum of conversation in the air. It was warm under her towel and comfy in her spot. She fell asleep, within minutes of resting her head on the chair. A bit later, she woke up just enough to hear Chris and Sarah talking about her. She decided to listen, eavesdrop, spy, whatever one might categorize it as. She was in a total daze.

"Thanks for a great time Sarah, the food as always was amazing." Chris said.

"You know you are always welcome Chris, I'm glad you were able to make it, after all."

"Hey, you aren't going to let her drive home, right? Can she stay the night here? I'll carry her to the guest room if you like."

Oh no, Katie thought, there was no way Sarah was going to let the opportunity to meddle pass on this one. However, Katie didn't speak up either. She didn't or rather couldn't move her head, let alone argue with either one of them. Katie also wanted to see how this played out and what Chris would do to save the damsel in distress. In typical fashion, Sarah never could leave well enough alone.

"We could do that. Although, Katie did mention that you guys made a truce today, so I'm sure it would be just fine if you take her home. Do you mind?"

Katie didn't hear a reply from Chris, but the next moment Sarah said, "Thanks, Chris, I'll get her purse for you."

Sarah knew darn well that Katie would be calling tomorrow to give her hell for letting Chris drive her home. Katie was in no position to say much at this point. To be honest, she was not even sure she could form words. It was more like a dream than reality. Hell, maybe it was a dream.

In this dream, Chris picked her up off the lounge chair and carried her to his truck. The only thing between her and him was a very small bikini, a beach towel and her rarely uninhibited mind.

Katie made sure she appeared to be out cold, the entire ride home. Chris propped her up, so she was leaning against him in the front of his truck, rather than the door. This was the closest she had been to him, in a decade, and she was not even aware enough to fully enjoy it. The truck jerked a bit going over a pothole, in the road, and she was moved a tad to the left. By the time they reached her house, she was practically in his lap.

Katie was fairly coherent when the truck stopped but she did not let on that she was awake. They sat in her driveway for a moment, and she could feel him looking at her, but she did not move nor did she speak. The swell of her breasts were exposed over the top of her swimsuit, even more than normal due to her position on the seat. It made her excited to know he was watching her, inspecting her body. She liked the heat of his stare.

Katie heard him fumbling in her purse and then the jingle of her keys. She heard the driver door open and felt the weight of the truck shift when his body lifted up and out of the vehicle. Her heartbeat accelerated knowing he would be coming around to get her. She didn't hear the driver door shut, so when the passenger door opened she twitched just a bit and almost gave herself away.

Instant goose bumps appeared on her arms and legs. She couldn't be sure if it was the air from the door opening or the anticipation of being in Chris' arms. Then he was lifting her from the truck.

She felt safe in his arms, and her body was hot despite the cool breeze whispering past them, as they walked up her driveway. Goosebumps in full flare up! It was as sensual as anything she had experienced, just to be pressed against him. Katie could feel his body reacting to her on the way to the front door. She had never felt so warm, practically feverish, while covered in goosies.

It took a minute for him to maneuver her in his arms and to open the door at the same time, but he made it work. The friction that was created as he juggled her and the door opening was the most excitement she had had in far too long. This was the first time he had been to her house and she hoped he was impressed.

Her home was a single story with a covered porch that extended the entire length of the front of the home. A pale blue picket fence looked surprisingly pleasant, giving a feeling of a miniature Georgian plantation home. Inside, there was an extra room for her to use an office and ample kitchen space. The kitchen was a little outdated with its green paint and décor, but Katie had found some accessories and knickknacks to make it a little more her style.

The stove was gas, a benefit for sure, just in case Katie had the chance to really cook or have guests. She had to have a gas stove and oven to do it properly. Lately she ate mostly salads on the go, but when it was a little more settled at work she wanted to start cooking for herself more. What really sold the place was the huge shower in a nice travertine tile that had a shower seat. Every woman deserved a place to perch and let the water drench her on long days and a spot for her foot to rest when she shaved. And people said women were hard to please, but it was really so simple.

You could smell the sweet flowers he had delivered to her the minute you opened the front door. He grunted with what sounded like approval and she wondered if he was pleased with her home. She did not want to let on that she was aware of what was happening, but it was becoming a challenge.

His arms wrapped around her, strong, and sure. His breath was warm and exciting as it touched her body. How he managed not to smell like chlorine, she could not fathom. Nevertheless, he did not. He smelt like summer. Like the sweetest memories of summer vacations at the beach, sunshine, palm trees, and freedom. This was killing her. When Chris found the bedroom, he gently laid her on the bed.

"What an awesome bed, Katie. Too bad we can't make use of it tonight." He murmured next to her ear. The sensation tickled in the most erotic way.

She loved this bed; its four posts were draped with a crimson red silky material, which drifted almost to the floor. Chris reached out and touched the fabric. Katie watched him through half open eyes. It was the kind of material that felt cool and slick along your body. Part of her wanted to tell Chris it was inappropriate to stand in her bedroom and look around, but she did not want to interrupt this moment.

She liked watching him, the way his body moved. It would be rude to scold him since he had been kind enough to help her home, so she justified to herself as she spied on him. There was also the small fact that she was enjoying it, of course. She closed her eyes quickly when his body started to turn back around to face her.

She thought she heard his pants rustle, but had no idea where he was in the room. Then she felt the bed dip beneath her, right by her left thigh. Then she heard the bed creak a little when it dipped yet again near her right arm. She could feel his breath against her neck, and even just that made her toes curl. He bent to kiss her forehead and she sat straight up in bed, knocking their heads together.

"Oh my God, I have to puke." Katie propelled herself off the bed, ran into her bathroom, and barely made it in time. Katie knew it was not conceivable to hope Chris was not hearing that she was losing the entire contents of her stomach. After a few minutes, Chris came to the bathroom door and gently called to her.

"Katie, sweetie, I'm going to come in and bring you some club soda for your stomach, okay?"

Katie did not respond. Talking was not an option at that point. He came in without permission. She was slumped over the bathtub and close to passing out. She didn't want to be near the toilet. She felt someone lifting her, but she was not really aware of much else.

Chris stripped down to his underwear and got into a lukewarm shower with her. Eventually, the water got so cold that it woke her up and she was finally mildly coherent. Awake enough to at least realize where she was and with whom.

"Chris, what are you doing here? Am I dreaming?" She was aware of him, his smell, and his touch and yet it did not seem real.

"No, sweetie, I'm really here, and as soon as you are a bit more awake I'll fill you in on the why." He held her close for a few more minutes, and Katie mumbled the whole time. Without realizing what she was doing, she began rubbing her hands across his chest. She seemed to find his nipples often, soon her proximity and touch were arousing him, at least it felt as though something was growing between them.

"Chris," Katie whispered, "I wanted to jump your bones the minute I saw you today, but shhh don't tell."

Chris responded with a throaty laugh and brought her face directly under the water. Katie squirmed a bit, but he kept her face there until she finally opened her eyes wide, and was awake enough to let out a little scream.

"What are you doing here, what are we doing together?" Katie was finally lucid and very surprised to see that they were standing in the shower together and he sure felt naked against her body.

"Don't panic, Katie. You had too much to drink, and I'm just trying to wake you up a bit. You passed out in the bathroom. Do you want to sit down for a minute in here and see how your stomach feels before I put you back into bed?"

"I feel fine, please, let me go."

The shock had yet to wear off as she had just been dreaming of him and now here he was for real. She was mortified. In her dream, she had been trying out his treasure trail and was just about to get to the goods when she woke up, his eyes staring directly at her. Chris turned off the water and set her on the commode gently asking her how she was feeling. She was okay at first, then her stomach lurched, and she knew she wasn't all right.

"Get out of my way," she said and pushed him aside a bit. She spent the next twenty minutes praying to the porcelain god while Chris placed cool rags on her neck and wiped her face. He brought her another glass of club soda and finally she felt like she could sit up without getting sick again.

"Honey, let me take you to bed and you can sleep this off, okay? I found some aspirin for you to take with your last few sips of club soda. Does that sound good?"

Katie really felt awful, but she hadn't thrown up in a few minutes, so there was hope she had gotten it all out of her system.

"Okay." Mortified! Her head ached, her stomach still felt like it was at sea, and she was at a loss for words. Okay, would have to do. She was beyond embarrassed for throwing up in his presence and mostly she just felt like she had been run over by a big rig. Chris took excellent care of her and made sure she was warm and tucked in for bed. He got her into pajamas, swearing he had his eyes closed most of the time, and even helped her brush her teeth before getting into bed.

She had always been a nut about brushing before bed and puke mouth was the worst way to wake up for anyone. He made sure she took the aspirin, had another tall glass of water and a trash bin at her side before finally kissing her forehead and leaving her to sleep. She dreamed of warm water, hot flesh, and soft tummy hair brushing against her abdomen. Mmmm... sweet dreams.

Chapter Five

When Katie woke up, she was more than a little confused as to how she had ended up in bed, let alone how she had gotten home. Her head felt like there was a punk band playing a gig right above her eyeballs. She stood up and almost fell, because her equilibrium was off, and then she tripped on her own pajama bottoms. She opted to kick them off to avoid further issues and found that she was not wearing panties. Eek!

Not caring what she was wearing, she threw on the bikini bottoms sitting at the end of her bed and headed to the kitchen. She needed coffee and a horse pill of an aspirin. As soon as she stepped out of the hallway, she noticed a pair of shoes sitting by the front door. They were men's shoes. Odd, she did not own any of those nor did she own a man, for that matter. Katie hoped that maybe with a cup of coffee things would start to make more sense.

She was in the kitchen when she heard the shower in her guestroom turn on and then what sounded like a man singing. Well, that would explain the shoes.

"Oh, my God," she said aloud, "I brought a man home last night and I don't even remember. What did I do?" She sat in her breakfast nook and tried to recall whom she might have brought home last night.

"Okay," she started going over the night aloud, "I was at the BBQ, and I know I drank too much wine and then we ate dinner. I remember the pool and the hot tub and then I think I sat on the lounge chair for a while. I certainly do not remember bringing home a man. Good news: he was in the guest room, so how inappropriate could the night have been. There were only a few single men in attendance. If it was the guy from Tom's work she would be humiliated.

"Ahhhhh!"

Five minutes later the coffee was ready and the water to the shower was still running. Sitting at the table she vaguely remembered being in the shower and for some reason, she was certain that she had not been alone in there. She remembered a hairy chest, not too hairy but soft, and that it felt good against her belly. Katie was so intent on trying to figure out the rest of her evening that she did not notice when the water stopped. Katie also didn't hear the guestroom door open or the footsteps down the hall.

"Oh please, don't let it be the guy form Tom's work!" Katie repeated to what she thought was her empty kitchen.

"Sorry to disappoint you honey, it's just me." Chris said and when she looked up from her coffee cup he had the most wonderful, sexy, mischievous, jackass smile on his face.

"What the hell are you doing here?" Katie questioned, and she wished she had taken the extra time to put her robe on or at least something other than her small bikini bottoms and her pajama tank top. Somehow, in this more intimate setting, it felt a lot like being naked in front of him. It might have something to do with the fact that Chris was standing before her in a towel and presumably nothing else.

"You are so welcome for my services last night, thank you for the appreciation." He was still smirking at her and she was none too pleased with him.

"Thank you Chris for getting me home safely, but what are you still doing here? I was fine, so why did you stay?"

"You think you were okay, huh? Do you remember me having to put you under the shower to wake you up?" Katie blushed and suddenly remembered a bit of the night's activities. "Do you remember puking for almost a half-hour while I applied cool rags to your neck and face? I wasn't sure you were okay, so I stayed in the guestroom last night to make sure you made it through the night. By the tone in your voice it's obvious that I'm not welcome here, so I'll get dressed and leave now."

He looked somewhat pissed. The truth was that she was grateful for his care the evening before. She remembered the cool rags, the gentle touch and a feeling of safety, even though she still could not see his face in the memories.

"Look Chris, I'm sorry for being so rude. I have a headache and I just wasn't expecting to see anyone at all this morning, least of all you. Please, sit and have a cup of coffee. Would you like some toast? I think that's about all my stomach can handle this morning."

Katie kind of thought he looked like the cat that ate the canary when she invited him to stay, but it didn't matter, it was the polite thing to do.

"A cup of coffee would be great. So, am I better than that guy who works with Tom or are you disappointed to find it's me?" Chris asked, "What was his name anyway?"

"I don't remember his name," Katie said through a laugh, "and I take the fifth on the other question."

She poured him a cup of coffee and left him to make the toast while she went to put on some decent clothes. She thought she heard a soft knocking, but did not think anything of it until she stepped into the kitchen and saw Sarah at the breakfast nook with Chris, who was still wearing only a towel.

"Hi Kates, I was just stopping by to make sure you were feeling alright this morning, but by the looks of things," Sarah looked at her and then directly at Chris when she spoke again, "you are doing just fine."

"It's not what you think, Chris was just helping me out last night. It's not a big deal." She knew the conclusion that was being drawn, and damn Chris for not trying to set the record straight.

"You don't have to explain anything to me dear, you are adults. Anyway, here are your sunglasses; you left them at my house last night. I have errands to run, so I'll let you guys get back to your breakfast, or coffee, or whatever." Sarah got up from the table and winked at Chris. The gesture did not go unnoticed.

"Let me walk you out, Sarah," Katie offered. When they were at the door, Katie took Sarah in close and said, "I know this looks bad, but nothing happened. He slept in the guestroom and I didn't even know he was here until this morning."

"Katie, you don't have to explain anything to me. I know that even if something did happen, you wouldn't see that you never stopped loving him. I don't know if you'll ever see that truth. Can I just say woman to woman: if nothing happened with you and that gorgeous man in your kitchen, it's a damn shame! I would imagine he can do all kinds of wicked things to make a woman swoon, and if you were smart, you would go in there and try to get a little before you scare him off."

Sarah practically floated off her porch and blew her a kiss as she got into her car. It's a good thing she left quickly, because Katie really wanted to pull her hair for acting so smug. Where did Sarah get off saying she had never stopped loving him? What did she mean she might scare him off? She had not been in love with him since she left this town. Of course, she didn't still love him that would be ludicrous.

Okay, honestly, it was a little bit after she left town that she got over him, but she wasn't still in love with him. How could she be, she didn't even know him anymore. She watched Sarah pull away and decided she was just letting "matchmaker" Sarah get to her and should drop the whole thing. Sarah was just plain wrong.

When she turned around and saw Chris standing in her living room with nothing on but his towel she nearly swooned. His chest all exposed, eyes sparkling, lips upturned in a smile, all of it made her breath catch. For a moment, she thought Sarah might be right. In that instant Chris must have noticed something change in her, because he took a step towards her, and then the toaster popped and the spell was broken.

"Sounds like our toast is ready." She wondered if he noticed her walls going right back up as she walked past him and into the kitchen.

"Toast… right." He sighed in response.

She refused to let Sarah get to her, there was no way she still loved Chris. How pathetic that would be. He probably had two more Amanda's waiting in line and hadn't thought of her at all, in the past ten years. After everything that happened, the last person she could be with was Chris.

They ate the toast in silence, except to ask for the butter or jam to be passed. It was uncomfortable, and Katie didn't know how to make it better. When they had finished, they sat there staring at anything but each other. Finally, Chris spoke up,

"This is really awkward. It's so funny, seeing as how we were inseparable once and deeply in love. Why is it that we can't even hold a conversation now?"

"Well, for one thing, you are half naked and that makes it a bit odd. And…it's been a long time. We were in puppy love Chris, we can't be expected to behave the same with one another. It's just different, and nothing can be done about that."

"Puppy love, is that what it was? Wow, things really have changed, haven't they? In my memory, you are the first, the only, love of my life. The girl who changed everything for me and to you it was some forgettable little crush. That is just great, Katie. I'm glad to see that some things haven't changed. You are still the only person that can make me feel completely inadequate. Thank you for making this easier on me, because now I can leave here and not worry about whether or not we can be friends. It's very obvious that we can't."

Chris got up from the table, with his towel half falling off and stormed into the guestroom. He made quick work of changing his clothes and was quickly in the living room getting his shoes on. She got the impression that he wanted away from her, and fast. He didn't even look at her and had the door open to leave, but before he could step out onto her porch, Katie stopped him.

"I'm sorry, Chris. I have disappointed you and I didn't mean to do that. I'm not sure what you want me to say and I don't seem to say the right thing when I do talk so…" her voice trailed off and she just looked at him.

"Katie, just tell me what happened. When you left, there were no calls, no explanations, just an empty space. Why did you leave me? You never even called or let me know where you were. Do you even know how badly that hurt? You broke my heart and I didn't even know why. Moreover, to hear you call what I felt for you puppy love is like a slap in the face. Maybe that's all it was to you, but not to me. I know it was a rough time after he died, but all I wanted to do was be there for you. I wanted to take care of you, what did I do to deserve that treatment?"

"Chris, please let's not do this. I don't want to talk about what happened. It was a long time ago and there's nothing more to say. It was painful and it's taken a long time for me to learn to live with the guilt and anger. Please let's just drop it and maybe we can even be sociable at parties or around town. I'll even be nice to your girlfriends." Katie half smiled at him hoping he would return the gesture, but he did not. In fact, he looked angrier.

"Katie, I don't want to be fake friends with you, which is what you are asking me to do. If we can't be friends then we don't need to pretend in front of the town. I wish you would tell me what happened that made you so angry with me. You never once talked to me after that night. I had to hear about what happened from other people. You broke my heart and here I am trying to beg you. Fuck that! I'm going to leave now, because this conversation only seems to get worse." Chris stepped through the door and from the porch Katie could hear him say "Girlfriends...I don't want anyone but you." What was she supposed to do with that knowledge?

Katie watched him speed out of her driveway and down the street. Why did this one thing have to ruin her new life here? Everything else was so great, work was going so well, and she was thriving in Pennsville. She had reunited with Sarah, who continued to be an amazing friend, and she felt almost at home.

She wouldn't let her feelings about Chris run her out of town again, but she couldn't let it stay the way it was either. She would see him around town, all the time, and they couldn't just ignore one another. She didn't know what she was going to do about Chris, but she knew she needed a bubble bath to soothe her mood. Sitting in her bath, she wondered how Chris was dealing with their conversation.

Chris was furious the whole ride home and when he finally arrived he apologized to Lady, his mocha colored, short hair cat, for not coming home and then he went straight to his bathroom. He needed a cold shower to numb himself a bit from the storm brewing within. The whole time he was undressing, he was telling Lady all about his fight with Katie.

"Then you know what she had the nerve to say to me, Lady? She said we could not be friends, but maybe we could pretend in front of everyone else. The nerve of her. Why would I want to be her friend after she called me her puppy love? I know, Lady, I couldn't believe it either..." Eventually his voice faded into the shower. Lady just sat on the countertop waiting for her master to finish ranting and take his shower.

Chapter Six

*D*ays passed and Katie was more and more upset about her night and conversation with Chris. She remembered a few more moments of the night; they were disturbing and thrilling all at the same time. She was almost certain that she ran her hands over his body. The memory was so prominent in her mind. She could remember the feel of his hard chest and the softness of his hair beneath her fingertips.

When they were younger he had very little chest hair, but even then, he had the makings of a treasure trail. She had never really liked hairy chests, as a teen, but then again not many teenage boys had them. When she was with Chris, many new things had appealed to her, like being goofy. She was never really playful until she met Chris and she couldn't remember being foolish since leaving him. In the last moments before sleep the night he brought her home, she remembered his tender lips on her forehead. They were firm, comforting, and safe. She was lost in her thoughts of him, when Paul cleared his throat, and woke her from daydreaming of times when she received more than friendly pecks on the forehead.

"Did I catch you at a bad time, Katie?"

"Oh, no, I'm sorry Paul. I guess I was daydreaming. Don't tell my boss, okay?" Paul had expressed concern about Katie for the past couple of weeks now. She had been caught more than once not paying attention and she had been losing her train of thought often.

"Katie, as the friend I hope I am, after the past few months, please tell me what has been on your mind lately. Maybe I can help or offer some advice. Heck, I'd even settle for just being a sounding board." Katie was not sure what to say to him and so she simply shrugged her shoulders in response.

"Ok, let me try this, as your boss, I'm concerned with your behavior, because it is definitely affecting your work. So, either talk to me or talk to someone else. Either way, please figure out what is wrong, because I need you fresh for the preliminary trial next week in the Riley case. We need to start off strong and keep the momentum in our direction, the whole time. I need you to be on top of your game, so I'm sending you home right this minute to rest or do whatever it is that you do to feel better."

"Paul, I'm fine. I certainly do not need to go home already. It's barely 3 o'clock and I have a ton of stuff to do still."

"I said go, and you have fifteen minutes to leave. When I come back you better not be here, young lady."

His voice was stern, but she could see the compassion in his face. She knew he must really be worried to send her home early. As he walked out of her office, she said,

"Thank you Paul for caring about me professionally, and as a friend. I will be out of here in fifteen minutes and when you see me tomorrow, I promise to be better. See you tomorrow." Katie put a smile on her face for him and he smiled back before leaving her office.

She didn't feel any relief to have the day off, because now she had to try to occupy her mind, which was not an easy thing to do. Usually work was an all-consuming task for her and when she wasn't working, she did not know what else to do. She could go home and read a book, but she was sure that wouldn't work either. Just in case, she tried Sarah on her cell phone, because school had been out for twenty minutes.

"Hey, Katie."

"How did you know it was me?" Katie quizzed.

"I have your work number programmed into my phone, so it pops up at me when you call, I believe it's referred to as Caller ID!"

"Ha Ha!" Katie snottily replied.

"Is something wrong, honey? You don't sound so good."

"What is it with everyone today? I'm fine. Paul kicked me out of work, because he insists there is something wrong, and because I have been lacking in attention a bit."

"Then there must be something wrong, because you are never lacking when it comes to attention span, especially for work. I take it you are calling me because you need some sort of distraction, from whatever is that is *not* wrong with you, correct?

"That is exactly what I need, a distraction. Got any ideas?"

"Well, I can think of a few that you would be upset at me for even mentioning, so how about if you come hang out with me and the kids this afternoon. I promised them we would finger-paint. If that isn't more fun than you have had in a long time, then I don't know what is."

Katie just snorted a laugh and agreed to be at her house in a half-hour. She needed to go home and change into more suitable finger-painting clothes, than a suit.

It took her a short time to freshen up and get ready to paint. She was wearing shorts and a ratty old mens T-shirt that would do nicely for painting. Her legs were long and lean and although not tanned, they were still attractive. She had always been fair skinned, and though she despised her coloring, she did not have the time or real interest to tan. Her breasts were ample and she was slim and curvy in the right places. It felt good to be out of her work clothes and in something that was more comfortable. This old town was affecting the new her, for sure. An afternoon with Sarah and the kids might just do the trick.

When she arrived at Sarah's she could hear the group in the backyard. Not only did Sarah have her kids, but also three of the neighbor kids were there, as well. They were spread out along the grass with cardboard canvases and each one was already a mess. Sarah looked thrilled to have her help.

"Thank heavens you are here. I think I am about to go nuts. Can you keep an eye on them while I go get the herd a snack?" Sarah was a wonderful teacher and mother, and Katie envied her for just a moment as she watched the scene.

"Sure, I can handle a few kids for ten minutes while you make a snack." Sarah got up and thanked her for the help. "Hey, what is the snack today anyway?"

"PBJ's without crust, crackers shaped like gold fish, and chocolate milk. Why, you want a snack too?"

"Yes please, that would be the best meal I've had all day, maybe all week. Thanks, Sarah."

"Anytime, sweetie, holler if you need help. They can get pretty rowdy!"

Sarah had not been kidding. She found herself more than once settling a petty argument over the paints and had to explain why they shouldn't paint themselves. You would think the older kids would try to guide the younger ones. It was in fact the exact opposite they seemed to think it was funny to get the younger ones to eat the paint, or throw it, or do pretty much anything they were not supposed to do. It had only been five, maybe ten minutes, but Katie needed Sarah to come back before things got worse. Apparently being able to hold her own in a courtroom did not necessarily translate to being able to control a few kids under the age of ten.

"Sarah, are you almost finished? I feel a mutiny coming." Before Katie even finished the sentence, she saw a paintbrush out of the corner of her eye headed her way. Within a minutes time she was almost completely face painted. The kids had all conspired against her and painted her hair, her face, her legs, and managed to spill the brush water all over her, as well. She could not help but laugh, so hard in fact, she thought for sure that she would wet her pants with more than just brush water.

"Snack ti… oh my word, what happened?" Sarah asked as she stepped out into the backyard. "What have you done? Oh Katie, are you okay?" Katie was sprawled on the grass, when she sat up and flashed a huge smile at Sarah, and they all broke out into laughter.

Sarah had a dishtowel in her hand and offered it to Katie, who was laughing so hard she was crying. The kids were already over the whole thing and moved onto the snacks, but the two old friends could not stop laughing and soon it turned into giggles. When they were kids, they often got in trouble on sleepovers for being loud, usually because of their giggle fits. Katie was wiping the paint from her face and trying not to eat anymore paint than she had due to her laughing, when Darren entered the backyard.

"Hey, what's up sis?" Darren asked.

"Hey kid, what are you doing here? Shouldn't you be at basketball practice or home?" she answered back.

"Well, I would be at practice except that Coach Staller has been a real bear lately and a few of the guys didn't show up for practice, so he just cancelled it all together and said we should all just go home and get our homework done. To avoid that as long as possible, I thought I would come over here, get a snack, and beg to go for a swim. Although it looks like I am not the only one who needs to dunk themselves in water."

"Oh," Katie said, "the kids decided it would be funny to paint me rather than the cardboard. It's startling how strong they can be when there are so many of them."

Darren looked at her and smiled with that look that says in simplest terms "You are a dork" and honestly, she felt a bit silly with the paint all over her, but she had laughed so hard that it didn't matter. It just felt good, to not feel bad. The kids brought her PBJ, crackers, and a few even gave her a hug thanking her for playing with them.

It felt wonderful and she realized for the first time that she was completely jealous of Sarah's family. She had great kids, a caring, albeit workaholic husband. Along with the little brother who liked to pop in all the time. It must feel good to have all that love and connection with people. All she had were books and work. She was lost in her self-pity when she heard the wooden side gate creak.

"Sarah," a deep voice questioned, "are you out here?" Then Chris stepped out into the backyard and looked straight at her, sitting there covered in paint. "Oh, hi Katie, I didn't mean to interrupt anything. Sorry, I'll go." Sarah stood from her patio chair and spoke up in protest.

"Don't be silly, Chris, you are always welcome here. What brings you by this afternoon?"

"Well, actually Sarah, I came to speak with you about something personal. But, it can wait."

Katie stayed in the lounge chair watching Darren play with the kids, rather than face the man she had not been able to get out of her mind for weeks, months, maybe even years. If she was going to have an honest moment, it was a decade. She reasoned actively, not thinking about someone, wasn't that much different from thinking of him in the first place.

"I'll call you later or stop by another time. It's really not important, so I'll just leave. Hey Darren," he called out with a wave, before he started to walk back to the side gate.

"Hey Coach, what are you doing here? Am I in trouble or something?"

"Not that I know of, Champ, I'm just here to talk to your sister about something. I swear it has nothing to do with you. Sorry again about practice, I guess I got a little too upset. I seem to be doing that lately. I promise that next week my patience will return. Have a good night."

"Night Coach, and don't worry we are all entitled to a bad day or week, besides, it meant I got to have a little fun on a school night."

"Are you sure you don't want to stay for a snack, Chris?" Sarah asked trying not to be too obvious without much success.

"No, thanks. I think that might be too uncomfortable. Night Sarah, night Katie," Chris turned around and headed for the side gate to leave. Soft enough so the kids couldn't hear her Sarah voiced,

"You are a damn fool, Katie Wright, if you don't chase that man down and make whatever it is better."

Katie wasn't sure what to do, because it depended on what she listened to, her head, or her heart. She did not want to walk on eggshells whenever he was near, but she didn't want to get too close to him either. The strange thing was that for the first time she was not sure if that was true. Why was she really avoiding him? Was it truly, because she could not get over the past? Because she wasn't so sure anymore that excuse rang true.

Katie leaped out of the lounge chair and ran to the gate that led to the driveway. Katie had no clue what she would do if he was still out there, but she couldn't let him go without talking to him. She was not sure what she would say after 'don't' go', but she would wing it when she found him.

Chapter Seven

*K*atie could not see his car when she stepped out into the driveway and immediately felt miserable. He left too quickly, and she wasn't sure she would have the courage to say anything to him, the next time they ran into each other. She went back to sit with Sarah and the kids for a while. Sarah was polite enough to leave her be, she didn't ask any questions as they cleaned up the paint play area in silence. Darren had the kids in the house washing up for dinner. Sarah decided to take them out to pizza, because she was exhausted from her day.

"Katie, would you like to come with us to get some pizza? I don't want you to be home alone tonight, you seem so sad. Please, come with us?"

Katie didn't really feel like a family dinner out, but she didn't want to go home to her empty house either.

"Oh, come on, my Mom and Dad are coming with us too, since Darren is already here. It will be loud and obnoxious, and you'll probably end up with pizza sauce all over you this time." Sarah was trying so hard, Katie felt as though she should go.

"Okay, I'll go, but I need to go home and change first. I'm a total mess and although I imagine you are right about the pizza sauce, I don't want to start out with the paint and give the kids any ideas." Sarah just smiled and shook her head at her.

"Okay," Sarah said, "Tom should be home in about a half-hour, would that be enough time?"

"I can handle that, I'll be right back."

She left Sarah and the kids to change her clothes. She really wanted to take a shower or better yet, a bubble bath, but she didn't have the time. She would have enough time to change and brush her hair and then it was off to a family dinner. Only it was not her family, and that was a bit depressing. She was almost thirty, with no kids, no husband, and no date or prospects in months.

Katie was lonely, she admitted to herself as she turned the corner to her street. She was a workaholic, who used work to get her kicks, because she could not find a man. She was two houses down the street from her rental when she saw a strange car in her driveway. A sports car of some kind, but she didn't know much about cars. Who had time for cars, or hobbies, or learning about new things? She was always working.

She had made herself completely depressed by the time she pulled into the drive. She looked on her porch and saw him there, rocking in her swing. It didn't matter how many years had passed. Her heart raced every time she saw him.

"Chris, what are you doing here?" She asked stepping out of her car and walking towards her home.

"I drove around a while, furious with you, and I just found myself at your doorstep. I knew you weren't home, so I figured I'd wait for you here."

"Well, I guess it's good I came home early," she stated.

"I would have waited all night."

When she looked into his eyes, she knew he truly would have waited, all night.

"You are crazy," Katie shook her head and with a nervous chuckle said, "Would you like to come inside?"

She wasn't sure if it was a good idea, but whatever was about to happen she knew she didn't want her nosey neighbor to see it all unfold. Katie opened the door and turned on the living room light. She was nervous and she hated it, because she rarely got nervous about anything, and especially not about men. However, Chris was different, he had made her uncomfortable since that first night at the basketball game.

"Would you like to have a seat in here or in the kitchen? I can make coffee; of course, it is a little early for coffee, but how about some juice or soda? I don't know if you drink any of those things, so how about water?" Katie spoke a mile a minute and fidgeted the whole time.

"I'm fine, thank you. To be honest, I don't care where we sit either. Wherever you are most comfortable is fine with me." Katie was fairly certain she wouldn't be at ease, no matter where they sat.

"If you don't mind, I'd like to wash up a bit, get the painted clothes off before we start." Chris just nodded his acceptance, "It will only take me a minute, please make yourself at home." With no further comment, she left the room and headed for her bedroom. Her first order of business was to call Sarah and let her know she couldn't make it to dinner. Sarah answered in less than three rings.

"Hello," piped her sweet voice.

"Hey sweetie, I just called to let you know that I can't make it to dinner."

"Come on Katie, what changed since you left my house? You had better get your butt over here right now. I refuse to let you stay at home, alone tonight. Hurry, okay? Tom got home early."

"I'm not home, *alone*, and that's why I can't make it tonight."

"What are you talking about, who's there?"

"When I got home, Chris was on my porch, waiting for me. I'm going to change and see what he wants. He seems like he won't leave even if I ask nice, or tell him I have dinner plans, so I figure I'll see what he has to say."

"Oh my God," Sarah hooted, "I can't believe he was waiting for you on your doorstep. Okay, you can get out of dinner, but only if you promise full details tomorrow. Deal?"

Katie knew she would be calling first thing tomorrow morning to get the scoop whether she agreed to the deal or not, so it was just easier to agree.

"Okay, I'll call you with all the details. Sarah, I'm so nervous around him, and I don't know why or what to do about it, this is going to be rough."

"What do you mean, you don't know why? He's a gorgeous man who is intelligent, and honey, he seems to want you *bad*. That would make any girl, who felt the same about him, nervous."

"You are crazy, he doesn't want me, he said he is furious with me and I sure don't want him."

"Then why was he waiting on your door step? Why did he take care of you when you puked your guts out? Why are you nervous every time you see him? Why do your eyes light up when he enters a room and your breath catches? Moreover, why did you run out of my backyard this afternoon to chase him? Honey, you both need to just let it out and have some hot sex."

Katie could not help it when a loud laugh escaped at Sarah's last remark. She only hoped Chris had not heard the outburst.

"You are truly a nut, and as nice and innocent as you look, you are a total sex freak. We are not going to have sex and we are not hot for one another. It's just a bunch of old feelings that never got resolved; besides, he dates cheerleaders and girls named Candy and Mandy these days, not stuffy lawyers."

"Jealous?" Sarah inquired with a snicker in her voice.

"Kiss my ass," Katie said with a laugh. "I have to go shower, but I'll talk to you tomorrow."

"Don't forget to shave your legs, men really hate stubble when they wrap your legs around them." Sarah was on a roll and was laughing so hard Katie thought she heard a snort.

"Goodbye, Sarah."

Katie had to hang up before it got any worse. She spent only a few minutes in the shower and did not bother to do anything but brush her hair. She was having a hard time deciding what to wear for this occasion, especially since she didn't really know what the occasion was.

She settled on her favorite boxer and tank top pajama set, the one she used for lounging around the house. She did not bother with make-up, but then again, it was not a date or anything. She kept telling herself that they were just going to talk. She put on some lip-gloss at the last moment, stepped out of her room, and went to have the big talk.

Chris was sitting in the kitchen, had set the table for two, and was pouring himself a glass of juice.

"Would you like anything to drink while I'm getting my own?" He acted as if it was completely normal for him to be in her kitchen.

"Um, well, actually, I would like some water, but I can get it myself." Chris motioned to the table and said, "I'll get it, just sit down." He got her a glass of water and sat down at the table.

"Are we having dinner?" Katie asked gesturing toward the set table.

"I thought you might be hungry and my stomach was grumbling, so I ordered pizza, if that's okay with you?"

"Actually, my stomach was all set on pizza tonight anyway, so that is fine. Thank you for the consideration."

"I'm a considerate guy," he said with a smirk, "you smell great, by the way." The comment made Katie warm and her whole body blushed in response. There was an uncomfortable silence, for a moment. Katie kept her eyes on her water glass to avoid Chris' eyes, which she could clearly feel on her.

"It's just lotion, but thank you. So, why did you come here tonight Chris?"

She looked up and met him eye to eye. Katie needed to feel more comfortable, and for her, that meant being on the offense and not the defense. She just went for it and hoped the lack of comfort would switch sides.

"I wanted to talk to you, but now I'm not sure where to start. I guess I just want to know why you seem to detest me so much."

Katie was a little taken back with his blunt question.

"What are you talking about? I don't detest you. I may not want to hang out, or go grocery shopping with you, or anything, but it's not like I hate you."

She knew the grocery store line was childish and snide, but it had just slipped out. She could not figure out why it bothered her so much that he dated bimbos.

"Well, I don't believe I have asked you to go grocery shopping yet, but now I know not too, right?

However, I have asked you to be my friend, to talk to me, and to share with me the things that made you go away from me all those years ago. I have asked you to be my friend and you have refused. That leads me to conclude, that you do not think very highly of me. I want to know why."

"Maybe it's all about me, did you think of that? Oh wait, I forgot one of my favorite traits of yours, conceit. I don't want to talk about those things because I don't want to be sad and I don't want to remember the past. Maybe I'm tired of being angry with myself, and guilty, and angry with you, and angry with everyone who had a part in that night." By this time, Katie was standing by the table and yelling, "There's no one for me to blame, because the driver who killed him died too. So, I blame me and I blame you and that makes it too hard to sit with you and talk about it all, because *you* helped *me* kill him!"

She could not believe what she blurted out in the heat of the moment. She had not meant to tell him that. She had never wanted to admit that she blamed him for that night, almost as much as she blamed herself. It had been so hard afterwards to look at him and not feel angry and/or guilty. She wouldn't talk to him or even make eye contact the few days she did return to school, after the accident.

"You blame me for your father's death? How... why... what did I do that makes me responsible for his death?" Chris looked stunned.

Before Katie could say another word, the doorbell rang and they both just stood there looking at one another. A minute passed and the doorbell rang again.

"Aren't you going to get dinner?" she asked when he did not make a move, at the second ring.

Chris left the kitchen without a word. She could hear him talking to the delivery boy and was thankful for his timely arrival. Things were going very badly. She had never meant to say any of those things. This was exactly why she did not want to talk about the past. From it came nothing good. It would only hurt her and Chris, and as much as she kept denying they could be friends, part of her wished that it wasn't impossible. She felt like crying, maybe she would, but not until after Chris left. She didn't cry in front of anyone.

Katie heard Chris come back into the kitchen. Her back was to the doorway and she didn't turn around until he spoke.

"Pizza's here, are you still planning to eat with me?"

Silence...

"Yes." Was Katie's arduous response to his question.

They sat in silence for some time trying to avoid eye contact. Katie got up and poured herself some more water, she felt like a robot, as she moved around the kitchen and then she felt a hand on her thigh and froze.

"You missed some paint." Chris stated as he scrapped a streak of paint off the back of her thigh. His hand felt warm and even though it was wrong, it felt nice to be touched by him. He finished far too soon and her thigh felt cold when he took his hand away.

"Thank you," Katie said breathlessly and turned to look at him. He caught her hand in his and they could not look away from one another. Katie willed her body to move away from him. It was too close, and there was so much to be said, now that she had bared some of her soul to him.

Chris' eyes begged her to say something. She felt like he was waiting for her to say that it was not his fault. He wanted her to take back what she said about blaming him for her father's death. She was sure that he didn't know what to make of her confession. No one would, she suspected.

"Katie," Chris whispered, "please tell me what's going on here. Explain to me how I'm responsible for a drunk driver hitting your dad that night. I don't understand, and I want to be clear before we go any further. I want you back in my life Katie, so please tell me, and trust me." She could not handle the pleading of his words and the way his eyes implored her. It was too much.

"Chris, I can't do what you're asking of me. I never should have said anything. Please, you should just leave. I have ruined any chance we had of being friends. It's too late Chris, and we both need to accept that."

Chris was furious, she could tell by the glint in his eye that he would not go quietly. Then his eyes calmed and he moved close to her and grabbed her as she tried stepping away from him. He pressed his body against hers, and then moved her so she was trapped between him and the kitchen counter.

"I don't know what it is that you hold over me, after all these years, my sweet Katie, but I haven't been able to get you out of my mind for the last ten years. I have dreamt of you and ached for you so many times. Do you even care that when I saw your face in the crowd that night, at the basketball game, it was as if someone had jolted my heart? You were beautiful, much more so than the image of you, I had saved in my memory. Darren said your name and I thought he must have been wrong, why would you move back to town? I was so confused and since that day, not a moment has passed that I didn't want to see you, or touch you, or even just hear your voice say my name. I want to make love to you even now, even after you just called me a murderer, and I can't explain why. You are driving me crazy."

The whole time he was inching his face closer and closer to hers. She tried to move herself away from him, but could not. She was trapped, not only by him, but also by her emotions. Soon his lips were a hair's breath away from hers.

"I have loved you since I was seventeen, Katie. I'm afraid I will never get over my first love, so I'm going to kiss you goodbye and hope maybe it will stick this time. You have the choice, as to whether it's goodbye forever, or not. I won't seek you out again, but if you feel even a bit for me as I still feel for you, come to me. I know we can work things through. I believe in us, I hope you can too."

Chris pressed his lips against hers. She gasped in disbelief, and although she was slightly resistant in the beginning, he nibbled and tugged at her lips until they parted for him. She was shocked, at first, by his tongue probing her mouth, but soon Katie returned his passion and feverishly kissed him back.

Stroke for stroke their tongues explored each other's mouth. It felt so familiar and yet different, more grown up maybe. She could feel the heat of his body as it pressed against hers, and it felt like the hot sun on a day at the beach. The moment you get out of the water and lay on your towel, as the sun caresses your skin and wipes away the water droplets. That was what he felt like.

Katie suddenly wanted to know what it felt like to be with him in the shower again, wet and half-naked.

On second thought, completely naked, and lucid this time, uninhibited this time. The thought made her frantic for a deeper kiss. She was on her tiptoes and she pressed her body firmly against his groin. She could feel his arousal grow with every kiss. Her nipples peaked against her shirt, begging to be touched. Her breasts had not ached this way in years, and it was exhilarating.

Chris must have felt them warm and piqued now pressed against his chest. Suddenly he deepened the kiss, his excitement evident in the guttural moan that escaped his throat. Katie loved knowing that she affected him, that moan made it plain as day that she got to him. His kiss was like the best sex she had ever had. God help her, she wanted the chance to explore more.

Katie heard a groan from deep within her escape, and felt Chris' physical response to her groan, against her belly. He was extremely gentle as he stayed firmly pressed against her, and she was delirious with his kisses.

"Chris…" she only had the chance to mutter his name before Chris picked her up and placed her on the counter, where she was closer to matching his own height. Suddenly, she could not remember what she had to say in the first place. Before she knew what was happening, Chris had her tank top on the floor and was cupping her breasts in his hands.

Chris was using his thumbs to play with the firm, pink bud of her nipples, his hands then moving to cover her breasts and caressing them firmly, but painfully gentle. She was about to beg for him to pull harder on her nipples, to grab her breasts with the fierceness she felt in that moment, when he took his mouth from hers and slid his tongue around her areola, and her ability to speak left her completely.

He smothered her areola with his warm breath before covering the left, then the right bud, with his mouth and tugging them sweetly with his teeth. At first, it was the anticipation of his mouth on her nipples that made her wiggle on the counter, but then his mouth was devouring them in turn, and she could not stand the pleasure. She was responding to him with moans and the occasional groan. She was moist from his touch and wanted more than anything for him to take her now, where they were. Right on her countertop, suddenly, having him inside her was the only thing that mattered. She needed him, wanted him, now!

Chris must have sensed her sudden urgency, because he slowly moved his hand down her body to settle between her legs. He touched her and looked up at her with such hunger in his eyes, that she got a little nervous. Then he smiled. The smile of a man very pleased to discover that even through her boxers she was hot and wet. He moved his mouth closer to her, and just before he brought his mouth down upon her lips, she got nervous.

"Chris, please… please," she could not manage to get out the rest before Chris was once again covering her mouth with his. He stroked her tongue with his over and over. Katie tugged at his bottom lip with her teeth and the sound that he made was more animal, than man, in nature. It spoke of raw need. He sounded desperate. To Katie's dismay, Chris pulled away from her. He looked her in the eyes and through gritted teeth managed to speak.

"When you can admit what we have, come to me," and then he turned around and walked out of her kitchen.

Katie was in shock and could not move. She heard him open the front door and then close it behind him. Katie hopped off the counter, pulled on her tank top, and on wobbly legs walked to her front window. Watching him unlock his door, she saw him take a deep breath before getting in, and driving away. She was glad to know that she was not the only one that felt weak and out of breath.

She was insulted and embarrassed that he had left her half-naked, in her kitchen. Quickly, her embarrassment turned into anger as she walked into her master bathroom for another shower, she needed to sit on the shower seat and think. She cursed the day she met that man and the day she decided it was a good idea to move back to this damn town.

Chris arrived home and stripped down before he got into his room and immediately jumped into the shower to take care of his problem. Later that night, he thought about calling one of his friends with benefits, but he was not in the mood for sex with any of them. He wanted Katie; he wanted to make hot, sweet love to only her.

Chris lay wide-awake feeling very frustrated, and yet a little bit more hopeful that he had awakened something in her, that would lead her back to him. She wanted him, he knew that for sure now, because a woman did not react that way to a man, unless she felt something for him. He just hoped she had the courage to face the past with him and clear the way for the future he knew they could have.

Ever since he set eyes on her again, he knew what had been missing from his life all along, Katie Wright. The love of his life, the keeper of his heart and the guardian of his soul, she was all of that. Her return had woken him up and the last thing he wanted was to go back to life without love, without family. That night he dreamed of a future, that he never even knew, he always wanted. A future filled with long nights of lovemaking, kids all over the house, and a wife with whom to grow old. He dreamed of the love he had once lost, but he hoped he would not lose again. He hoped she was lying awake unable to think of anyone but him. It served her right, for the torture he felt.

That night Katie did not get a moment of sleep. She tried to convince herself that it was only sexual frustration, which made her react to Chris the way she did. The fact that she had not had sex in more than a year was the cause, as far as she was concerned. She just hoped he did not think it was anything else. It would never be what is used to be for them, so there was no point in thinking it could. But in her dreams, everything was even better than they had been as teens, and there they made love all night.

Chapter Eight

*T*he next day Katie was even worse off than the day before. She tried to play it cool at work, but it was not working that well. Paul kept looking her way, during the brainstorm session, about a new hit and run case. They were certain that the suspect had committed the crime, instinct told them that, but they could not place him at the scene, and he had an alibi for the time the accident occurred.

He was at a bar, according to less than spectacular witnesses, and made a call from that bar thirty minutes after the accident to report his car stolen. It was more than feasible that he ran back to the bar after the accident, and then waited a few minutes to call in the theft. It was actually ingenious, considering he was drunk when they went to take his report.

The whole meeting Katie tried to pay attention, and she even had some good ideas as to how to work around some of the witnesses, but she was not herself. She was hoping to sneak out before Paul could corner her and ask her what was wrong, again. Little did he know she was even more upset than yesterday. It seemed she was not capable of getting Chris off her mind.

She had dreamt of him all night. More than once, she woke up aroused. The dreams were so vivid and when she rose from bed in the morning, she felt like she had been up all night having outrageous sex. Reality had made her gloomy all day and she couldn't shake the feeling that she had made a horrible mistake. She was thinking of him then; the way he had kissed her, the touch of his hand on her breasts, the heat of his skin against hers, and it was more than she could handle, more than... The sound of a book crashing to the table startled Katie and made her jump in her seat. She looked around to see everyone was gone, but Paul.

"Katie, I've said your name at least three times without you responding, once. Everyone else left and you didn't even notice. Please tell me what the hell is wrong with you, because I need to be able to count on you during these discussions, and when we go to trial. I can't have you spacing out on me during important trials. I mean, shit, what can I do? Please tell me."

"I am so sorry, Paul. You are right, I have been very unprofessional the last few weeks, and I apologize. I won't let my personal life interfere with work anymore. It's just been hard coming back here and I didn't think it would be this tough, I'm so sorry." The last few words were said through tears and only at whisper level. Katie could not help herself and began to cry.

Paul moved closer to her and gently put his hand on her shoulder for comfort. In her desperate state, she leaned against him for a bit of support. Paul seemed a little uncomfortable at first, Katie knew from stories around the office that he did not do well with crying. He always said he was a father figure, so Katie was counting on that, and hoping he had come to think of her in the same light. He sat there with her for a few minutes until the crying quieted.

"Katie, I know that we work together and I am your boss and even though it hasn't been that long, I have come to think of you in a daughterly way. What I'm trying to say is that if you need someone to talk to, I would be more than happy to take off my boss hat, and just be a friend or a mentor. Whatever you need just tell me please, I really can't bare it when people cry."

"Oh, Paul, it's about a boy and I feel so stupid saying that. It's about a boy who I have loved since I was in high school and all of a sudden, I feel horrible, as if we just broke up yesterday, even though it's been ten years. I know we have never talked about my dad, but when he died my mom and I ran from this town. Here we are in a meeting talking about a drunk driver case and I can't focus. You know how much these cases mean to me. That night when my dad was hit, well it changed everything for me. Oh, I'm all mixed up and confused. I've been running from the memories of my dad, of the accident, and I'm also running from Chris.

He was there, with me, that night when the deputy showed up to take me to the hospital. I don't know what to do, I mean, I think I might still love him, but at the same time, I'm scared Paul. I miss him, even though I don't really know him anymore. Does that make any sense?" She hadn't made much sense at all to Paul, she was sure of that.

"You know, more than once I've heard the tale about your father's accidental death, and the quick departure you and your mother made to leave town. Everyone always said Chris was devastated when you left. I saw the tension between the two of you at dinner. How you both tried to catch looks at each other when no one was looking. It reminded me of times when I had to hide my love for Helene.

Once, we were engaged to be married, and not to each other. We were in the same group of friends and ended up losing all of our friends to be together. Sometimes love is risky and you have to fight many obstacles, but I can tell you I would do it all again, for the life I have with my wife. At the time, it was very hard. It took a long time for us to admit our love for one another.

Katie, I don't exactly know what is going on here. I'm not even sure that you do, which may be causing you some of the trouble. However, I do have this to say about life in general and my life specifically.

There are few things in life that I regret. And I have found that it's not the things I have done that I regret, but those things I was too afraid to do, that I find I could kick myself for, even now. A life without taking chances is no life at all. No matter what you decide or how it turns out, please do remember that. Take chances, be brave, and always when it comes to love go for it."

Katie nodded her head and looked down at her hands. Paul got up from his chair and started to straighten up the conference room, waiting for her to speak, it seemed.

"Thank you for talking to me, and I promise I'll get this all straightened out in no time, and I'll be my old shark of a lawyer self again soon. I will be ready for the Riley hearing, I promise. Thank you." She did not know what more to say, it had been years since anyone gave her fatherly advice and she wasn't sure what to do next. Paul came over and gave her a gentle hug.

"I'm going to try this one more time. Go home now." He probably saw she was about to argue, so he stopped her right away, "No, not a word from you Miss. You are taking today and tomorrow off and I will hear nothing about it. As far as I'm concerned, you are feeling ill, and need to rest. It's not that far from the truth and you know it, so that is that.

You will take this time to relax and figure out what's going on with your personal life, so that you can come back and kick ass professionally. With the weekend that gives you four days to get back to normal and then you'll be full steam ahead. Now, what are you waiting for? Go!" He was practically pushing her out the door and she knew she would not win, if she contested.

So Katie turned to Paul and simply said,

"Thank you for caring, this time it will work. I swear it's a miracle you don't just fire me instead." She managed to fake a smile.

"Don't thank me; they're your sick days, after all." He said with a knowing laugh.

Katie left the county building and hoped that when she stepped back into her office, four days from now, she would know what was happening to her and have a hold on it all. It was not like her to cry and be such a girl about things. It had been a long time since she had been weepy and emotionally distracted. Maybe, she thought to herself, it was because it had been a long time since she allowed herself to feel, period. Now all she had to do was figure out what to do with herself, for four days.

It was clear that she needed to get out of town, but her Mom's house was too far away for a four-day trip. Instead, she decided to take a trip to the coast, Cape May, and stay at a bed and breakfast that had recently sent her a post card offering special rates. She was in luck, they had two rooms left for the weekend, and since she was a new customer, the owner upgraded her to a view room for the weekend.

The owner, who answered the phone, seemed very nice. Katie got the impression that it would be a great place to spend some time alone and think. She needed to figure out what had been happening to her the past few weeks. Moreover, she needed to do it before Paul lost faith in her. Before she left, she had one stop to make.

◆◆◆

On the other side of town, Chris was having just as much trouble focusing. He had gotten little to no sleep the night prior. The day was dragging along and he was not sure whether he would be in good enough shape for the basketball game he had that night. He played in an intramural team, among the local community members, all sponsored by small businesses. It was not an important game exactly, because they were already in the playoffs, but every game counted to him. The more wins the better.

He had missed any shot at the pros, thanks to his knee injury in college, but he could play with the other old guys around town and make a bit of a show of it still.

His last year in college he was scouted by football teams and a few basketball teams had showed interest in seeing him play. He was having a tough time deciding which one to choose but it turned out the choice was not necessary, after he was hurt.

At the end of the second half, he was taken down by a free safety, after catching a high ball in the end zone. The kid; upset that his team was losing, and a hot head anyway, grabbed Chris by the helmet and when they fell, they were all twisted up together. Chris, unfortunately, was the most twisted, including his leg, which was facing the wrong direction. The other guy stayed there while Chris tried to push him off, talking trash into Chris' face about how he would get him again, and how Chris was nothing he couldn't handle. When he finally pushed the punk kid off him it was only the sight of him puking, at the shock of Chris' knee, that made him forgive the guy.

The kid was only a sophomore and his aim had been to look like a big bad boy for hitting Chris so hard. It was all about ego back then, and Chris had been that boy once. In an instant, his dreams of going pro were gone. Instead, he went through physical therapy for the rest of the school year and finished college with good grades. Another scholarship, from a generous alumnus, helped him to finish his masters and become a teacher.

It was a shock when he had to change paths midstream, but it all worked out in the end. He was a good teacher, loved this town, which was still odd to him, because he had always been trying to get out and leave it behind as a teen. He had a good life now. Everything was great until Katie came home.

When he saw her that night at the basketball game he really had felt like the wind had been knocked out of him. It was like seeing a ghost, but the most beautiful of ghosts. He had resolved himself years ago that she was gone forever and that night, just for a moment, he thought maybe he had been given a second chance.

Chris knew right away that he wanted to get her back into his life. He told himself on more than one occasion, even before she accused him of murder, that he was nuts. He didn't even know her anymore. How could he still be in love with her? She was practically a stranger, but there were parts of her he knew well, and those were the parts that he had been dreaming about for ten years.

Over the years, Chris found himself dreaming of her every few months. She was the one woman he knew he would always love. He had been in relationships with other women but it had always been about sex and fun with them. With Katie, even when he was dreaming, he woke up with more sense of fulfillment than sex, with anyone else, had ever provided. Chris now cherished those first moments when he woke up, because although they were fleeting, he got to feel love and then reality would hit him and he always felt empty.

She was the only person who had ever known all of him. To everyone else he showed bits and pieces, the parts he felt most secure in, but with Katie he wanted her to know all of him. He missed her, plain, and simple. He missed who he was with her; he was better with her, better than he ever imagined he could be.

The bell rang and he recognized the fact that he had neglected to pay attention to the kids, and the boys were harassing the girls who were playing basketball. They usually played co-ed games, but with basketball, he found there were always problems playing co-ed. He usually ended up with at least one girl bleeding from a guy knocking her down to get to the hoop.

Alternatively, he would get boys with bruised egos or bruised eyes, because they had gotten too close and touchy feely with a girl. Most of the girls were not afraid to kick butt. Kids were trouble, but he loved his job anyway. He scattered the kids and got them inside their respective locker rooms, so they could change back into their school clothes.

What he wanted more than anything was to go home and hide, but he knew he could not do that, so he went in to get ready for the next batch of rowdy kids. He only hoped he could clear his mind long enough to make it through the end of the day.

Chapter Nine

Chris made it through the day and even managed to give, what he thought was some good advice, to a student and player of his. The kids tended to seek him out for advice on all sorts of issues. Many of the teachers were opposed to his being so close with the kids. They told him it was not his job to be the student's friend or confidant, but to teach.

He always felt like teaching meant life lessons too and he, unlike many of the other teachers, was not afraid the kids would turn on him. Many of his co-workers were afraid to trust the kids. Chris had managed to do all of the above, and in some ways, he knew the kids respected him more.

On his way to the office, he saw one of his football kids hanging all over his girlfriend in the hall, and spoke up about it.

"Cooper, have a little class and respect for your girl, will you? At least wait until you get her into the car."

Cooper gave him a "yes sir" and a nod while the girl blushed three shades of red. Cooper had stopped pawing her out of regard for Chris. He hoped he would turn that into respect for the girl, if he gave it a little thought.

Chris liked to teach them lessons without them realizing he was trying to get them to learn. Sometimes, it was the only way to get to teens, especially the teenage boys. Not much could compete with sports and girls.

"Hey Rita," Chris said when he walked into the school's front office, "How was your day today?"

Rita was the office secretary and Chris pretended he was blind to the fact that she had a major crush on him. He was as nice to her, as he was to all of the staff at the high school. The only problem was that Rita seemed to take the friendly behavior as flirting and he often feared it gave her some small hope.

"Hi there, handsome," she was trying a new bolder approach hoping he would notice, "Who brought you the love-note today? Did you get a new girlfriend without telling me?" Rita was not very good at subtle.

"I didn't get a new girl; as a matter of fact, I think I am swearing off all women."

"Well, I'll make sure to tell the woman who came in today to leave you alone, if she comes in again."

Rita was smiling as big as she could and trying her best to give Chris the come-hither look. He was more interested in the note that was neatly folded in his mailbox. It was overly feminine in a lavender hue and inlayed with flower petals. Unfolding the note, the glorious scent of strawberries wafted up to his nose and he would swear there was also a hint of champagne, and he instantly knew who dropped off the letter.

"So, sexy, I was thinking that maybe we could go out sometime and see if there is more than flirting in our future, what do you think?" Chris didn't even hear Rita speaking to him, "Chris... hello... earth to Chris, are you there?" He just kept sniffing the note and looking at it like it might bite, "Chris, what is the matter with you?"

"Oh, sorry Rita, I've got to go, but have a nice day, okay? See you tomorrow."

Chris walked away from Rita without ever noticing that she had finally asked him out on a date. Chris would never have gone out with her anyway, because she was his co-worker, first of all, and she was not his type by a long shot. Even with his friends with benefits, Chris had strict guidelines, and Rita just did not fit them. He liked much more confident women.

He loved Katie, and at this point in his life he was not going to settle for anything less. All he could focus on was the note in his hands. It was small paper and that worried him, because the only time she had ever written him a short letter was when she had been mad at him. Her love notes were always long; she was just that sort of girl. The scent was so mild that it must have been unintentional, so he didn't think this was a lover letter.

He wandered his way over to the nearest bench, in front of the school, and with one final sniff of the note, he said a prayer, and opened it up. This could be the end or the beginning, he thought.

Chris –

> *I realize, as I sit here, that this is the second time I have written to you, like a coward. Except, last time I didn't even have the nerve to give you my goodbye letter. I was still a bit of a child and even today, I guess I am still a bit of that same girl who has lost her way.*
>
> *Then, my mom thought that things could never be the same, and that the only thing to do was leave. I was so angry then, angry with myself, and angry with you, it never would have worked.*
>
> *Now, I find that I'm stuck again and I don't know what to do about anything. I only know that after last night I simply cannot face you and say what I need to say. You made everything more complicated last night. You made me want you when I swore I didn't. You made me feel things I swore I no longer felt. It's all too much between you and me. I'm leaving for a few days to*

think and figure out what's true and what's hormones. You always did have the ability to arouse in me this carnal need to feel my body against yours. That has not changed. When I return I'm not sure that I can give you what you want. It may be that we will have to politely avoid one another. I'm sorry that things cannot be simpler for you and me. Just know that I'm sorry for calling our love puppy love. I will be honest with you, and myself, and say that it was the truest and most amazing love I have ever felt, and nothing has ever compared to that. I suppose that's the way it is with first loves; they are always the most tender, the most intense, and always the most painful. Please know that I have always cared for you and I hope we can be friends in time.

Always, Katie
P.S. Thank you for the flowers, Charming

Chris was torn apart when he finished the letter. She told him he made her feel things she thought were over between them, and in the same breath told him that they might never be friends, and then she said she hoped that they could be friends.

"She is so confused," Chris, said to the air, "Now she just confused the hell out of me!" He stalked around the school for a good fifteen minutes just thinking about Katie. Thinking about what to do when she did return, and what would happen if she did not want to be more than friends, or not friends at all.

There was little time to ponder the letter, because basketball practice was starting and then he had his own game to attend. He needed this practice to relieve his mind from thinking for a bit.

He found focus in teaching some of the younger kids the basics and helping the varsity team with their fancier moves. He had two kids who could dunk and he didn't like them to show boat that talent too much in the game, but he did love to watch them in practice. They were all great kids and he wanted the best for them. He was a walking, talking, billboard for why these kids should have school and good grades behind them. If he had slacked like most of his teammates in college, he would have been much worse off when he was injured.

School saved him, and he always told his kids that. His standards for the team grade point average where higher than the school districts, and although it was not completely enforceable, so far none of the parents had challenged him. The kids gave him peace and even tonight, they managed to distract him a bit.

It was not until after his basketball game that night, which they won 98-86, when he again pulled the letter up in his memory and tried to figure out Katie Wright. He was on his way to the pizza joint they frequented, after every game, and found himself so distracted that he went the wrong way and was late.

"Shit Chris, we almost sent out a search party. Bob saw you turn left at Meadows and since we all know that is not a through street," laughter from the group, "we were wondering what the hell happened to you." Little John made this comment and laughed heartier than anyone else.

This was one of those occasions when they called him little because he was big, not because he was small. He was usually the first to take a shot at one of the people on the team, and interestingly enough, he was not actually on the team, but somehow was always there.

"Have your laughs John, but just remember who the real tough guy around here is," Tom, Sarah's husband, stood up and said, "I believe that Chris here saved you from the very scary mouse that invaded your house." With that, everyone roared with laughter and John sat down.

"That should keep him quiet." Tom whispered to Chris, "At least until he thinks of someone else to make fun of tonight."

"Thanks for the rescue, but it wasn't necessary. I know why he picks on me and if it makes him feel good, that is fine.

Besides man, I was totally out of it the whole ride over here and I got myself all out of whack. It was a loser move."

"Let me guess what's wrong. Could her name be Katie Wright?" Tom questioned and nudged him with his elbow.

"How did you know… ah Sarah, right?" Tom nodded his head in confirmation, "So, does Sarah know what the hell is going on with her?"

"She just mentioned to me last night that Katie cancelled dinner with us because you showed up at her house. Sarah was excited, because she has been hoping you two would hook up since Katie came back into town. Anyway, Sarah was a bit upset because Katie was supposed to call this morning to tell her what went down, but she didn't. I guess Katie finally did call and said she would be gone for a few days, but when she got back, they would talk about it all. Sarah was really hoping you had swept Katie off her feet and gone to Tahiti, but I told her that was probably not the case, since we had semi-finals tonight. Do you know where Katie went?"

Chris only shook his head in response.

"I wasn't too happy either." Chris said and then got quiet.

Tom kept talking, because it seemed that Chris only wanted to listen. He went over some game points and asked a few questions on strategy. It was getting uncomfortable and luckily, they both had pizza to chew on which gave them an excuse for the lulling conversation. Tom and Chris were not exactly good friends. They were acquaintances and ran in similar circles due to Sarah being a teacher and a shared love of sports.

When Chris asked if Tom knew the story of him and Katie, he could tell he surprised Tom. He was probably even more surprised when Chris offered to share the story with him.

"Oh, um okay, sure. Just let me order another beer." Tom got his beer, and with that taken care of, Chris started to tell the tale of the day his life changed. Tom sat patiently and listened to every word while Chris poured his soul to a man he barely knew.

"She changed my life from the moment we first spoke. The whole day had been unusual from the start. I was on time for school, got a decent grade on a pop quiz, and the principal let me slide into chemistry class just past the bell without giving me a detention. For me the day was already much better than most, but when Katie asked me out it was as if suddenly for once life was treating me well. She doesn't know that I know this, but she was trying to ask my then best friend out, and not me.

Circumstances as they were she made a mistake and I got the date, not John. It was the best day of my life, up to that point. I had been lusting after her since the first day I saw her walking onto the high school campus. She was remarkable, even then. She walked around as if she could care less what people thought of her and it was fascinating to me.

I was so afraid of people, of myself. Rocking the boat was not my thing. Plus, she was smart and beautiful. Not in an obvious way, like some of the flashier girls, but in a quiet unknowing way. Over the next year and a half, she changed my life. One date led to another and I think she was more surprised than I was to find that she loved me.

She made me strong and gave me a reason to believe in myself. She encouraged me to be better, to try harder, and soon it started to pay off. All of a sudden, I was doing well in school, started to excel in sports, and even managed to get a scholarship to college. I was popular for the first time in my life.

It was her greatest gift to me and probably what caused her the most grief. With my new confidence and success around school there was a new popularity, and that meant girls were more interested. Katie did not handle it well and, well, I didn't either. I think it was even harder for her, at the time, because we were each other's first lovers. She gave me that gift and I barely kept that special.

There was no one interested before Katie, but during and after Katie, there was never a lack of women. I can be honest and admit that things were getting bad between us before her father's accident. After the accident, she would not let me in, and soon after she left. No forwarding address, no phone call, nothing, just gone.

She broke my heart, and I didn't even know how much she mattered or how much I truly cared until she left. That's our story, short version. It was intense and incredible and all too quickly it was gone. I like to think I added something to her life too. Katie was always too serious, she had no idea how to be goofy or have fun. I think with me that changed.

I have spent the rest of my adult life comparing every woman to Katie, and no one has ever stood a chance. The moment I saw her at the team's first basketball game of the season, it was as if time had melted away, and I was instantly in love again. It was that same intense kind of love that only happens the first time, smack in my face, all over again. Now I don't know what to do, because she won't even talk to me about the possibility of a date, let alone admit that she loves me still. I know that she loves me." Chris took a deep breath and looked at Tom, "got any ideas?"

Tom looked uncomfortable with the entire discussion, and Chris was aware that it was not standard procedure for his friends to discuss relationships in this detailed a manner. Men were not as comfortable giving advice as most women. Man code suggested it was best to stay out of it, but he tried to implore Tom to say something with physical cues, sort of like puppy dog eyes, but much more manly.

"All I can say, man, is that you don't seem to be the kind of person who gives up on anything, and Katie is definitely not the kind of woman a man can let go of without a fight."

Chris nodded in agreement and took a sip of his beer as he thought, "If only Katie saw the man I am now and not the boy I was then, maybe she would find me as hard to let go of as I do her."

Chris and Tom switched topics and moved closer to the crowd, and although Chris was quieter than usual, he managed to get through the night with the team. It was only when he got home that his heart ached and he found himself again lost in thoughts of Katie. If nothing else, he knew he needed to do something, because every day being without her seemed more painful than the last.

Chapter Ten

*M*ore than three hundred miles away, Katie was finishing dessert at the B&B. She had tried to be a bit social after dinner, in the parlor for coffee and light dessert tray. Nevertheless, she knew she was not good company, so she took her leave of the group and headed to the front porch. The B&B was beautiful and at night, sitting on a swinging porch, she almost felt relaxed.

She sat on the swing and looked out over the ocean, which shined in the moonlight. It was actually very romantic. The realization that she was alone made her sad and she almost began to cry, then the front door creaked open and she got her bearing. The owner of the B&B, Beverly, stepped out onto the porch.

"Everything okay out here, Miss Wright?"

"Oh, yes Beverley, everything is okay. I was just enjoying the beautiful night. And please call me Katie, it only seems fair."

"Katie it is then. So, what brought you to my place on such short notice?" She asked as she sat on the swing next to Katie.

"I just decided I needed to get away for a while, to a place quieter than my home."

"You know, anytime I have tried to get away from the noise, I have found that the noise was in my head the whole time. I hope you don't think I'm prying too much, but you look to me like a woman who could use someone to talk to, and perhaps it would help that I am removed from whatever situation you seem to be so consumed with, out here tonight."

"I really appreciated the offer, but I'm fine, thank you."

"I understand, just know that the offer stands."

"Thank you," Katie said with a sigh.

They sat there is silence for a few minutes, both waiting for the other to speak. Katie wanted to say something, but the only thing on her mind was Chris. She finally broke down and spilled to Beverly.

"I came here to get away from a man. I fell in love with him when I was sixteen. I should have known we were headed for disaster, but who can see such things in their youth? I was so wrapped up in him and the love I felt for him, I missed the obvious signs. Not to mention we were so young, who thinks rationally at that age, right? It all happened so suddenly... it was a mistake actually. I was trying to ask his friend, John, I think that was his name, on a date and inadvertently I asked Chris instead.

I even avoided him for almost a full week after asking him out; he must have thought I was a horrible person. My mother was so upset with me, because he kept calling and I kept making excuses not to speak to him. I was truly amazed when after our first date I was so enchanted with him. He was charming and I hadn't expected that, because he was so shy.

He made me laugh and when he smiled, I wanted to smile too. I don't think I fell in love right away, but it didn't take long. I saw in him something special, and I think I may have been the first person to tell him he was great. He was smarter than I expected and talented in ways, even he didn't realize. He amazed me, and when I fell for him, I fell hard. I guess the hardest part for me was that the more I helped him see what he could be, the more he slipped away.

All too quickly, he was attractive to most of the female population in school and I felt left out, let down and inadequate. In my haste to help him change I didn't consider that they might not all be changes I liked. He was fooling around with girls, thinking I didn't know, still telling me he loved me more than anything. It didn't seem possible to me that he could love me and still hurt me. I gave him all that I could and in the end, it wasn't enough.

At least it felt that way to me. We were having trouble and then my father was killed in an accident and without going into the details, I blamed Chris and myself. When my Mom and I left our hometown, I didn't even say goodbye and I thought I would never look back. I guess, to be honest, I thought of him often, but with the connection in my head linking him to my father's death, the thoughts never ended well.

Then a few months ago, I moved back to my hometown and there he was. It turns out that he moved back to teach high school. Seeing him has confused me and I can't seem to figure out why. He makes me nervous, and I feel a connection to him that should have been buried a long time ago. I guess that's why I came here. It all got to be too much for me and I needed some time to think and figure out what was happening to me."

Katie realized that she had babbled all this to a complete stranger.

"I'm so sorry Beverly, I didn't mean to lay all of this on you at once. You don't even know me and I just made you sit here while I went on and on about this. Please forgive me."

"Sweetie, there is no reason to apologize; I asked the question and offered the ear." Beverly placed her hand on Katie's and gave it a squeeze, "Katie, I think that you need to remember one thing about your past; you said your father was killed in an accident. Accident being the key word in that phrase, right? Maybe if you can forgive yourself for whatever you think you did, you'll be able to forgive your friend.

I want to offer you one thing to remember and then I will stop the mini lecture; a man only makes you nervous when you are afraid of him. Something tells me this man makes you afraid because he makes you feel. Sometimes love doesn't let you go, even if you think you have let go of it." Katie did not know what to say and just squeezed Beverly's hand in return and looked out over the ocean waves.

After a few days at the B&B, Katie was feeling better than expected. Her talks with Beverly had been therapeutic. She was almost ready to face Chris again. On her way home, she stopped at the office and went through some of the massive pile of paperwork that was sitting on her desk. It seemed everyone else had been very busy while she was away. It was almost time for her big case and she needed to focus. Paul was counting on her and she was not about to let him down.

Although she was feeling better about Chris and wanted to talk to him about the past and the possibility of a future, she needed to make sure that this case went well. By the time Katie got home, she had five hours before it was time to wake up, and get back to the office. Her vacation was definitely over and her Monday looked to be a tough one.

The next couple of days were a blur of work and little sleep. She did not have the time to call Chris, because she knew it would take a while to have the talk they were bound to have. Katie also thought the conversation deserved more than a phone call; she wanted to see him in person. After all these years, she was about to tell him how much that night affected her, why she left and that she didn't really blame him for her father's death. She realized now, and would explain to him, that she had blamed herself and it was just easier to blame him at the time. With the trial underway, it was just too hectic. She only had time to work.

They had all the evidence they should need for a conviction. Jury selection had been on Monday, and she and Paul got a jury in which they felt confident. Opening statements were on Tuesday, and by Friday, she was exhausted. The emotional toll a child abuse case took on those involved often outweighed the task of lawyering. Thankfully, Katie felt as though it was going really well and Paul was in agreement. That did not help her body from needing to collapse. The moment she walked into her house, she put on her pajamas, crawled into bed, and did not move until eight the next morning.

Her first order of business, waking up on the gorgeous Saturday morning, was to call her mother and tell her the results of her trip. She had been so busy she had not even had time to call her Mom with her big revelation.

She wanted her Mom to know that she had forgiven herself, and Chris, for the past. Her mother never could understand why she refused to speak with Chris after dad's death. She hated to discuss the accident, so she was a little nervous, but she knew her Mom would be happy for her. She would be relieved that Katie had let it go and that she was content with her life these days, almost happy. Talking about dad always made them both sad, but if they did not talk about him, then they were never able to enjoy the good times either.

She just needed to share the healing she had been doing with her Mom. She felt as if a weight had lifted and she knew her Mom would be thrilled. Mary had tried to explain for months, after the crash, that it had been an accident and she was not to blame. She kept telling her that when it was your time, it was time, and nothing could have been done to prevent her Father's fate. It was about time Katie saw the truth for herself. Her Mother answered the phone in two rings.

"Hello, Wright residence," she said,

"Hi, Mom."

"Oh, hi Katie, what a pleasant surprise. You are a day early for our weekly chat, I missed hearing your voice last week."

"How are you feeling today?" Katie asked.

"As well as can be expected, for someone whose most exciting activity for the day is getting her mail," to which they both chuckled, "I'm doing fine sweetie, but I'm a bit tired of this house."

"Mom, we have talked about this so many times. Why don't you look into volunteering with kids or taking classes during the day?"

"I know sweetie, I think I finally agree with you on that. It's time I stopped sulking around this house and got active. I guess I just needed to get to this point before I could take a step forward. I never used to be this meek, but maybe I'm making a comeback."

"That's great Mom, I'm so happy that you have changed your mind. I have done a little mind changing recently too, that is why I called actually. I've told you how difficult it has been for me here since seeing Chris at the basketball game."

"Yes, you may have mentioned it a time or five." Katie could feel her Mom's smile come through the phone.

"Very funny, Mom. He makes me so confused and I can't remember the last person who affected me this way. It's as if I'm instantly a teenager again when he is around me. Anyway, the weekend away has led me to some drastic conclusions."

"So, you are finally ready to admit that you are still in love with Chris?"

"That's not what I was going to say Mom, please just listen to me for a moment. I want to tell you about me, and then I'll get to Chris. While I was away, I realized that I have spent all these years blaming myself for what happened to Dad, when it was not my fault at all. I think I have forgiven myself for calling him that night. I get it, Mom, after all these years I finally understand that it was not me that caused his accident.

I blame the drunk driver for taking him from us, and I wish that life had dealt us a different hand, but I can forgive Chris and myself for that night. I miss him dearly, but I'm at a point where I can be thankful for the time we had with him and not dwell on the time we lost. I feel better than I have in ten years, Mom. Can you believe I finally feel free of all of that?"

"Honey, I think that is wonderful," her Mom said with sob caught in her throat, "I'm so happy for you. I have been trying to tell you for years not to blame yourself. I can't believe after all this time it only took a weekend away, to realize that you needed to let go of that anger. Please, tell me this means I may have a chance at a happy daughter who has more in her life than work."

"Let's take this one step at a time, okay? I'm ready to forgive, but that doesn't mean that Chris and I are going to date, it just means maybe we can be friends again. He seems to have changed a lot in the last decade and I'm hopeful that we can be friends and see what happens from there.

He told me that he wants to be in my life and insinuated that more was possible from his side, but I'm not sure how I feel about that. Just because we were in love in high school does not mean that it will work now. Please do not get your hopes up, or put any pressure on me about this." Katie used her stern lawyer voice so her Mom knew she was serious.

"I can't help it if I want my daughter to be in love and married with children, before I am too old to remember her name and have to eat Jell-O at every meal. I just want to see you out there in the dating world and not stuck at work every night. I promise not to bother you too often about this, but let me know how things go. I imagine that you are going to tell him your new revelations?"

"I will tell him soon, I'm just not sure what to say, at this point. We did not leave things very well and I'm afraid he'll refuse to speak with me. I'm also nervous about telling him what happened that night. I never told him why I was leaving or why Dad was on his way to get me. It all happened so long ago and I don't know how to bring it up after all these years."

"Katie, I'm sure he will understand when you tell him the truth. He was always a kind and understanding young man, and I'm sure that with age those characteristics have only grown stronger. Free yourself of this burden, honey, and find happiness whether it's with Chris or some other fine man. I just want you to be happy; it's been so long since you sounded this content."

"I feel great Mom, just great." They spoke on the phone for almost an hour about her work, Sarah and her family, and her Mom's new decision to get out of the house. Katie was hoping some fresh air and friends would get her Mom to a point where she could even make a trip to see her. Katie could not have felt better. Her Mom was moving forward and so was she.

The rest of the day went by quickly as she cleaned the house and then went into her office to review case files. Her stomach prompted her to look up at the clock, to find it was already eight at night. Her few days of rest put her completely behind at work. She was organized, almost to a fault, and needed to have everything ready to go to finalize her case against Riley.

She was very confident that the jury was on her side. More than once she saw one of them teary eyed while one of the young men testified about their experience with the defendant. She felt secure in saying she and Paul could have the prosecutions side wrapped up, by the end of the week. Feeling assured enough to leave the office Katie made her way home. She decided to take a day off on Sunday, she thought it might be a good day to try to talk to Chris. She hoped that she would have the courage to tell him everything.

When Katie woke on Sunday morning, she felt great. Everything seemed to be going so well. Work was wonderful and it was easy to have faith that after her visit with Chris, she would begin to mend their friendship, which she had cherished years ago. Even when he was turning into a jerk with a huge ego in high school, he was still the best friend she ever had.

He may have been a rotten boyfriend, but he was always there for her when she needed a friendly ear.

Katie was actually excited to see him and explain to him what a nice trip she had. She was still nervous about telling him the whole ordeal, but knew he would understand. Somehow, Katie just knew he would be there for her again, and the thought made her happier than it probably should. She realized that she missed him, after all these years she still missed him.

Katie spent extra time primping for her visit and talk with Chris. She felt the need to look her best for the talk with Chris. She knew that once they were face-to-face the words would fall into place.

It was still early, but she thought he would most likely be awake, so she decided to head over to his house. She knew where he lived, thanks to a quick email to Sarah earlier in the week. Everyone knew where everyone could be found in this town. Katie supposed that in this instance it was a benefit. She did not always feels this way, but today she was willing to accept it as a good thing.

Walking up to his front door, she was impressed with his home. Sarah mentioned that he bought the place a few years back and did most of the renovation himself. Except for the guys he bribed around town with pizza and beer to get some of the heavy lifting items done. The house was similar to Paul and Helene's, in that it was narrow and long from what she could tell. The garage was set back and detached from the main house with a long driveway down the side. It was beige with brown trim, to include that which was on the windows and the front door. She never would have thought to paint the trim such a dark brown, but it actually went very well together. The landscaping was well tended and there was more grass than cement or flower beds. Other than mowing, it was probably pretty low maintenance. When she had looked at every possible thing on the outside of the house to avoid walking to the door, she figured she better just do it before someone caught her and thought she was stalking Chris!

Walking up the walkway, to the stoop, was agonizing and after a deep breath, she rang his doorbell. No one answered, so she gave it one more ring. She could hear footsteps and got ready to greet Chris with a smile, because she was not sure that he would be initially happy, considering the way they had parted. When the door opened, Katie was more than surprised to see Amanda, standing in what was obviously one of Chris' shirts, and apparently nothing else. The look on her face must have been laughable, she was fairly sure her jaw literally dropped.

"Hi, can I help you?" Amanda asked nicely.

"Um, no," Katie stumbled, "I must have the wrong house. I'm sorry to have bothered you so early."

"Wait, I met you at the grocery store remember. If you are looking for Chris, I can go get him for you no problem. He was just getting out of the shower."

"No, that's okay, really. I seem to have come at a bad time. Don't even mention I was here; I'll get a hold of him some other time. Thank you anyway. Sorry to bother you. Amanda, right?"

Amanda nodded and started to say something when Katie cut her off as she turned around and with her back already turned said, "Have a nice day."

Katie high tailed it off the porch and practically ran to her car. She looked back one time to see the front door close and it seemed achingly symbolic to watch it shut, and in her mind, she heard the click and flinched.

◆◆◆

Chris was in his hallway when he heard his front door click, coming around the corner he saw Amanda looking concerned.

"Who was at the door?" Chris was in a towel, bare-chested, hair still wet from his shower.

"It was that woman we saw at the grocery store, I don't remember her name, but she remembered mine. What was her name again?" Chris instantly felt green, nauseous, pukey green.

"Are you okay, sweetie?" Amanda questioned.

"Katie was here and you opened the door. That's great, just great, boy am I screwed now!"

Chris went to the door and opened it, but she was long gone. He was hoping he would be able to catch her and explain, but how could he. He had claimed to want to start again just a week ago and here he was with another woman, who obviously had stayed the night. What if she had come over to talk and to make up? What if she had changed her mind and wanted to give them a chance? He may have just screwed up his whole life.

He was sure she was the one. He felt as though he had just lost his best friend or that someone had run down his puppy. Amanda must have been able to read the truth all over his face, because she guessed right away what was wrong with him.

"So, she's the one, huh? She's the reason you wanted to cool off and the reason why you called me all desperate for company. I was her stand-in?"

"Amanda, you were not a stand-in for anyone. I like you and that's why I called."

"Well, it looks like maybe she changed her mind, because she was sure disappointed to see me at the door. I understand the faded smile on her face, now that I see your face. Except you look worse than she did. You better find her and make this better Chris, or you'll never forgive yourself."

Chris felt bad that she was so on target, and didn't want her to think that she had meant nothing to him.

"Chris, sweetie," she said stepping close to him and touching his freshly shaved faced, "it was a pleasure to be your stand-in. We had fun, the sex was out of this world, and you make me laugh, I can't complain about any of that. It was a good time, but I'm no match for the way you feel for that woman. It's clear as day all over your face. I'm going to go take a shower and you should put on some clothes and find her. I'll lock the door when I leave and return your key under the mat."

"It doesn't have to be so quick Amanda, we can still be friends. It was fun being with you."

"Chris, I appreciate the gentleman in you coming out to make me feel better, but there is no need. I told myself the day you picked me up at the park not to fall in love and I actually managed to hold on to my heart. It would be easy to fall in love with a guy like you, but I knew from the start that we were only temporary.

Please don't feel bad for me, I had fun, but this is the end for sure. Something tells me if you get the girl, she won't appreciate a friendship between you and me, and to be honest, I can't blame her. I wouldn't trust any woman with you even if I trusted you.

If you don't get the girl, it would be too hard to be a stand-in for an actual person. It was okay when she was faceless. I can't compete with her in any category in your mind, I fear. Besides, I think it's time I found my own man to rope." Amanda stood on her tiptoes and kissed him sweetly on the cheek. "Good-bye Chris and good luck."

Amanda stepped away and walked into his room to shower. Chris waited until he heard the bathroom door close to go into his room for clothes. He could not think of anything else to say to her at this point. He knew she did not want to hear he was sorry and really she had said all there was to say. She had been very kind, all things considered.

At the moment locating Katie and finding out what she had come over to say was more important. God help him, he hoped she still wanted to say it and he hoped that she changed her mind. He wanted to be hers so badly. In so many ways, he had always been hers. No other woman had ever compared to Katie. Even as a girl she was ten times better than the women he had found since her, she was his one shot at a Happily Ever After. He lost her once, and he was bound and determined to get her back. He would not take no for an answer this time.

Chris tried Katie's house first with no luck, then he called her office, but there was no answer, and he knew there was no one to let him in if she was there anyway. He stopped by Sarah's with no luck. He was happy that they were not at home, so he did not have to explain why he was frantically searching for her around town. He did not know where else to look. He knew when they were kids, whenever she was unhappy, she went to the local ice cream parlor, so he tried there. He did not see her car anywhere, but he went in to check with Martha to ask if Katie had been in before him.

Martha had always been someone he could count on, ever since he was a kid. She was still behind the counter after thirty plus years. When he walked in, her smile was immediate. She had been a mothering figure to him for most of his life and before he even said a word, she knew.

"Well, it must be my lucky day Katie was just here, about thirty minutes ago, for a scoop. What a sweet girl, she was a might preoccupied, barely said two words and we both know that's not like her. I don't suppose the look on your face is about her, is it?"

"Funny you should ask, because I am in fact looking for her. I thought she might stop in here."

"I sure hope whatever you did you can fix, because that is the kind of woman I have been trying to get you to look for, someone to tame your devilish ways. Not those sweet, but dumb, rocks bits you bring in here from time to time. You need a woman who challenges you, who puts you in your place every now and then." She said with a soft chuckle and a smile that radiated with the motherly love she had for him. Chris gave her just a whisper of a smile before his face fell back to worry.

"Martha, let's just hope I did not screw it up again. Did she say where she was going, by chance?"

"Well, sweetie, she did ask me about that old swim hole where you kids used to jump off that rock. You know the one, by Willabee Bridge? I told her it was still there as far as I knew, so maybe she went there next. That's my best guess, kiddo."

"I know exactly where you are talking about, thank you Martha, you are a life saver." He grabbed a piece of toffee from the counter and took out his wallet to pay her and she shook her head at him.

"Just get out of here, my Chrisy-boy, go get that girl. It's about time you settled down."

Chris smiled and thanked her for everything. It took twenty minutes to drive out to Willabee Bridge and when he got there, he saw Katie's car and thanked heaven for Martha. He was nervous as he parked the car. He took a moment to collect his thoughts, before stepping out, and starting to climb the rocks to get to the swim hole.

It had been years since he had been to this place and the path was not nearly as easy to follow these days. The trees were overgrown and he was nicked, more than once, by a branch as he was making his way to the spot. There was a community pool with a giant diving board, so the new generation of kids no longer came out here to swim. Mostly, the boys had brought girls out here to impress them. Jumping from the bigger of the two rocks always did the trick, and then the goal was to make out, in the many hiding places that the trees provided. He could remember a few times that he and Katie had spent here not caring about anything, but one another.

She had always been a better jumper than he was. She was never afraid of the big rock and eventually got him up there, but it had taken a lot of convincing. She had routinely been very successful at convincing him to do most anything. She was not above using her feminine wiles to talk him into things. He always enjoyed the reward, and she usually made it better than promised.

They had a favorite spot for their make-out sessions here, it was back where the trees grew tall, but the sun had just enough room to shine right down the middle of them. They spent many hours lying in their swimsuits, on a blanket, kissing and talking about all the things they wanted to do after high school. She always forced him to think about the future. She said it was important to know where you were going, or else you would not be prepared when it was time to go. It did not make sense to him for a long time, but he played along anyway.

He made it to the top of the hill and he could see her lying in the sun. She did not notice him for a while and it gave him time to take her all in, piece by delectable piece. She was obviously not prepared for swimming because she had jumped in with only her bra and panties. Katie was gorgeous!

Set against the scenery of rocks and foliage, she looked a bit as he imagined the sirens of Greek mythology would. He had always thought tanned woman more attractive, but looking at her soft milky complexion, he could not remember anything more beautiful. She had the most adorable freckles across her nose and a few speckled across her body. Her skin shone with water from the river. She was gorgeous, and vibrant, and he was doomed!

When he finally got the nerve to say something he found himself unable to speak. He got closer to her and sat on the rock. He went to touch her thigh and she jumped. He had a feeling he was going to pay for startling her.

"Oh my God, Chris, you scared the shit out of me, I wasn't expecting anyone else to be here. What's the matter with you sneaking up on women, half naked, no less?"

She realized that she was exposing herself to him and wished she had had the sense to put her clothes back on right when she had gotten out of the water, but the sun felt so warm and therapeutic that she wanted to dry underneath its warmth. Katie went to reach for her shirt and found that it was farther away than she thought and she would have to stand up to get it, which would mean exposing herself to Chris even more. It was lucky that she had on navy blue under garments today or she would have been embarrassed. She just told herself it was like being in a bikini and went back to concentrating on Chris and why he had showed up to see her.

He was staring at her so intensely that she could feel warm spots whenever his eyes moved along her body. There was desire in his eyes and for a moment Katie remembered their kiss in her kitchen. It had been the most awe-inspiring kiss of her life, except for their first kiss. That had always been her favorite. She realized that they were sitting in silence and it was making her uncomfortable, because she was still mad at him.

"What the hell are you doing here, Chris?" Katie needed to break the silence and her anger was returning, as he sat there just staring at her. It was making her feel warm and sexy, which was irritating. She did not want to be warm from him, or feel desire for him, what she really wanted was to be pissed!

"I came looking for you, I went by the ice cream parlor hoping to find you, and Martha mentioned you might be here."

"I'll have to remember not to tell her where I'm headed from now on, because I came here to be alone, so please leave, Chris."

"Katie, please talk to me. Why did you come to my house this morning? Please tell me what you had to say."

"I told her to leave it alone and not tell you it was me, but I guess that was a silly request. She sure looks cute in your shirts; I can see why you keep her around." She knew she sounded jealous, but it could not be helped, Katie was upset, jealous, and angry.

"It's not exactly what you think Katie. Yes, she was there and yes, she spent the night, but it has nothing to do with you and me. Except for maybe that you have been home a week, and after that note you left I thought you would come to me, and you didn't. Why didn't you come to me earlier than this morning?"

"Oh, I'm sorry Chris; I didn't realize I was on a schedule. Forgive me for my tardiness. I should have known there was a five day limit on how long you can go without the adoration of a woman, my apologies!"

Katie hoped that Chris could tell by her tone that this was not going to be easy, he was going to have to work to get her to open up to him about what was on her mind.

"I'm sorry that you came over and saw Amanda there, but I won't lie. I'm glad to see that it bothers you a little. At least I know that you have some feelings for me."

"Yes isn't that fantastic? I'm glad you are so happy that I think you are a total jackass, that's great. Well, guess what else; I also think you are a liar and a big fat…ape." Chris could not help but smile.

"You think I'm an ape?" He started to laugh and the look on Katie's face got more intense and fuming the more he laughed. "I don't think anyone has ever called me such a despicable name before. Boy, you lawyers really know how to cuss a guy out, don't you?"

Katie was not amused with him and the more upset she got the more he laughed.

"You think you're funny don't you, or rather that I'm funny. I hope this is not your way of trying to get me to talk to you, because I'm pretty sure this is not going to work."

Katie crossed her arms over her chest and looked a lot like a child who had not gotten her way. She looked up at him and he laughed again, so she punched him in the leg.

"Ow-ah, what was that for?" Chris said still with a smile.

"That was for laughing at me, you jackass, now get out of my way. This conversation is over."

Katie stood up and began to walk to her clothes pile. She didn't care if he got the show of his life, she wanted to be dressed and get away from him. Before Katie got more than two steps, Chris had her by the arm and pulled her in close.

"Katie, don't walk away from me this time, please. I'm sorry for laughing I just thought it was cute and your reaction was even more endearing; I didn't mean to laugh at you, I swear. I just want to talk to you, please talk to me."

"Chris, let me go, I want to get dressed." Chris looked down at her, only a breath apart and Katie practically naked.

"You smell like lavender and rain." He whispered.

His breath gave her goose bumps up and down her arms. The immediate response by her body worried her. She didn't want his closeness to diminish her anger and warm her to him.

She pulled away to try to mitigate both his physical and emotional hold on her, but he did not let go right away. He rubbed his fingers gently over her shoulders and down her back, as if he was playing a soft piano tune. He moved her bra strap to its correct position, as it had been falling down her arm. Katie could feel a bulge pressed against her. He was about to kiss her when she tugged away from him and went to the pile of clothes.

"We can talk when I have my clothes on; it seems to be causing you some discomfort."

◆◆◆

Katie said unabashedly looking at his arousal. Chris would normally be embarrassed, but for some reason he was not ashamed of his reaction in this moment, to this woman.

"Don't expect me to be ashamed of my natural response to you. I have told you how I feel about you and it should be no shock that I find you sexy. Damn it, look at me Katie! I want you in more ways than just physically, but at least I'm honest with you about how I feel. Why can't you do the same?"

"I don't need a speech on honesty from you, Chris Staller. You don't know anything about honesty; if you did, then Amanda wouldn't have been at your house this morning. I do believe last time we saw one another you told me that you and Amanda were broken up, do you remember that Mr. Honesty?"

Katie was furious and it showed all over her face.

"Katie, it's not what you think, we'll it's not exactly what you think. I did break things off with her, like I said, but when I didn't hear from you well I got upset and I was lonely. I wanted to be with you, but I figured you must have given up on me, so I called Amanda and asked her to come over last night. I didn't intend for her to stay the night, but she usually does, and I didn't know how to tell her to leave politely. So, she spent the night.

You may not believe me, but all we did was sleep. She tried to start something when we went to bed, but I couldn't. Well, I could, but I didn't want to, so we just slept. I guess I just wanted a body in my bed. I'm not proud of it, but I'm being honest. Amanda knows about you, and she was very understanding about the whole thing.

She was never in love with me either, and we agreed that this morning was the last time we would ever see one another, no matter how things turn out with you and me. I'm sorry that you saw that, but it was not as bad as you think. Please believe me Katie, please tell me why you came over this morning. I have been looking for you all morning, to say…to say… I'm sorry. Katie, I'm truly sorry."

"Bravo, that was a nice try Chris, but you are exactly the same as you were in high school. I can't believe I was about to apologize to you this morning. You are a grown man. Surely, you know how you tell a woman to leave, you just have to use your big boy words. You are not a kid anymore. Don't try to charm me into thinking you don't know how to talk to women. You used to be scared of every girl in your path. I showed you how wonderful you were and then you took that and shared it with every other girl in school.

All of a sudden, you thought you were the best thing God ever created, and you stopped caring about our love, and me. It was all about you and being popular. You wouldn't even have been popular if it wasn't for me. I gave you the time of day when you were still just "John's friend."

Then, as soon as other girls started paying attention, it was as if I didn't exist. You think I didn't noticed how much less you would hold my hand at school or kiss me around other people? Of course, as soon as we got home you were all over me. Do you have any idea how that made me feel, Chris? I was in love with you and just wanted to be your girl. All the while, you were busy trying to make every girl, your girl.

Do you recall why my father was on the road that night? He was on his way to pick me up from that party we were at, because I caught you making out in the basement. I saw you with some slutty girl, making out, and it broke my heart. I called my dad crying, and he rushed to get me, but he didn't make it, did he Chris? No, he died on the way to save me from my joke of a boyfriend.

That's why I left town and never called you again. You broke my heart more than once that night, but the biggest loss was my father, not you. I can see now I was foolish to think you were different. Still using women to boost your ego, I see.

That's what Amanda was, right? An ego boost, because I didn't come running to you after my trip. You are so full of yourself and… and a big, fat, ape."

Katie was only half dressed, but she grabbed her shorts and shoes and stalked off paying no mind to Chris calling her name.

Chris let her go and sat down on the rock in defeat. On more than one occasion he had tried to get a word in, but Katie was not hearing him, she was like a mad woman. He could see the pain in her face, as she reminded him what really happened that night. He always wondered what caused her to cut him off so quickly. He did not remember the girl, the making out, or any of it really.

He did remember watching her get into the deputy's car, he remembered the tears running down her face. How could he have forgotten? The front page of the paper the next weekend was Katie and her Mom, walking down the steps of the church, after the funeral. She looked so heartbroken, refused to take his calls, and ignored him at the funeral service.

Now he understood what happened between them that last night at her house. She blamed him for the accident, and he couldn't say in all honestly that he was innocent in the chain of events. It was his fault in Katie's mind. He did not even remember that girl's name, but he did remember that it was not the first time he had done something like that.

Katie always had to be home early and he had kissed plenty of girls after taking her home, and returning to parties. He didn't think she knew about all that, he had almost forgotten it himself. He did not have any remorse at the time. He just knew that it felt good to have all the attention from the other girls. He loved Katie, if he had not he would have broken it off with her. There were many offers from girls to have sex, but he never went that far. Somehow, in his mind, that meant it was okay to kiss and mess around behind her back, as long as he saved her something special.

He saw now how naïve he was about everything then, especially women. By the looks of things, he was still screwed up when it came to women. It was possible that he had just let the best thing that ever happened to him walk away, with no fight at all. It would take a lot to get her back; but as he lay in the sun in the spot she had just been, he promised himself he would not give in easily.

He needed her for so many reasons, and he would make her believe in him again. He was different, and he would prove it to her, any way he could. She made him better, she always had, and he wanted to be a better man for her and for himself. She needed him just as much, and he knew it. Now he just had to make her see it too.

Chapter Eleven

*K*atie was relieved not to hear anything from Chris for the next few days. She had been very busy with the trial, she didn't need the distraction of him calling her, although she was surprised that he hadn't, she was glad all the same. She already spent too many hours thinking about him and each kiss. Katie's dreams were filled with him and his touches.

It was strange, because in most of her dreams he looked like he had at sixteen and seventeen. The touch was the same as it had always been, soft, gentle, and passionate. It was only while she dreamed that she felt comfortable with the idea of a life, with Chris. When she woke, there was only fear because she wanted him and emptiness because she couldn't have him.

The following Saturday morning when she woke from another dream about Chris, she could not help but cry. They were making love near the waterhole and just before she woke up Chris kissed her forehead and whispered, *Katie, I love you.* Katie finally pulled herself together and went running. It was nice to be out of breath and feel worked. Her career was rough, but she needed a more physically demanding sort of release. By the time she got home, she thought she might pass out on her porch.

Then, she noticed a package on her steps and knew instantly who must have left it there. Her hands were shaking as she picked it up and took it into the house. She wanted to blame the shaking on her long run, but knew it was anticipation that caused her hands to quake.

Opening the package carefully, she was taken aback by the beautiful gift within. She could not believe that he had spent so much, on a gift for her. After all, she had turned him down in no uncertain terms. She took the most beautiful tiara from the box. She could not help but try it on and rushed to the bathroom mirror. She looked at her reflection and a memory hit her like a punch to the gut. When she and Chris had been dating for about a year, she had a dream that they got married and in the dream, she had been wearing a tiara.

Looking in the glass, now a grown woman who had given up on those types of fantasies, a tear rolled down her cheek and she had to look away. She went back into the living room and placed the tiara in the box. She was not sure that she could or should accept such a gift, but she wasn't ready to face him and return it yet, either way.

As she closed the box on the tiara, a handwritten note slipped out from the top,

Your Prince has arrived

He hadn't signed the note, but there was no real need to. She knew exactly who sent the gift. How is it that he remembered the dream? It had been so long ago, and she had since given up on fantasy men and fantasy lives.

She sat on her living room floor for hours just thinking of what to do next. Katie alternated between crying and trying on the tiara repeatedly. She was in love with the little royal beauty, but knew it could not stay with her, it was much too expensive a gift. The diamonds were not huge, but there were enough of them that it must have cost him a small fortune.

It sparkled like vampire flesh in the sun atop her head, and it did make her feel like a princess, despite the fact that she looked a disaster from her run. It was simply, too much. She was nervous that she might have to see him again in order to return the gift. She could not believe that he had risked leaving it on her front porch. This was no bunch of flowers, someone could have walked away with it, and she never would have known. It was too much to handle, so she got off the floor and headed into her room for a shower and a nap.

It felt good to be in the steam and have the water wash away her worries. She used her lavender scented soap, it was supposed to be calming. Whether it worked or not, at least it smelled good. When she crawled into bed, she was actually able to sleep for a couple of hours, until her doorbell woke her. She was in a nap comma, so it took her longer than the person at the door wanted to wait, as was evident by the persistent ringing of the damn bell.

"Please, God," she said aloud, "don't let it be Chris." She was not ready to see him again and was more than a little relieved to find Sarah on the other side of her peephole.

"Boy am I glad it's you," Katie said as she opened the door.

"Well, I'm happy to see you too, but who did you think it would be?" Sarah chimed.

"I was afraid you were going to be Chris. He left a present on my doorstep today and I thought he might be stopping by to talk. Which I'm definitely not ready to do."

"Oh my, a present, what did he bring by, more flowers?"

"No, it's a bit more than flowers. It's actually way too much, and I'm not sure what to do with it or him at this point."

"Well, don't keep me in suspense, what did he drop on your stoop?"

Without saying a word, Katie went to the box and opened it for Sarah to peek.

"Oh my Lord," Sarah said with a gasp, "What in the world was he thinking buying you something like… like this? I mean if this is the kind of thing he does for a woman who refuses to even talk to him, what the hell does he do for a woman who admits that she loves him?"

"I'm not in love with him, why do you keep saying that?"

"Oh honey, you can try and fool yourself all you want, but I can see it in your eyes when he walks into a room. The way he makes you so "heated" all the time. The way you want to run every time he gets too close, except of course, when he is kissing you. You are crazy for him. I mean, my goodness, you get all hot and bothered just telling me about the heat between you two from a few stolen kisses. You two are better than one of those romance novels."

"You are totally exaggerating and wrong, because it was just a kiss. I'm not in love with him and this gift is completely inappropriate for our non-existent relationship. Was in love and is in love are totally different."

"Say what you like Katie, but I have seen the way that man looks at you and I could hear your heart beating the first time you saw him again. What is so wrong about admitting that you want to see what happens with him? What are you so afraid of, is it him, or relationships in general?"

"Sarah, don't be fooled by him. He wants me now because I'm saying no, but as soon as we give it a shot he would realize that it was the chase he was after and not me. Men leave Sarah, they all do. One way or another, they all find a way to leave."

"That is ridiculous Katie, if you really thought about it rather than letting your fears get in the way, you would know that. Not all men leave. Your father never would have left your Mom, never. You can't let fear get in the way or you will never be happy. What good is life if you are always waiting for the other shoe to drop? I have a happy marriage, but it's tough and some day we may give up, but that doesn't mean that my children won't have a Dad or that my marriage was a bad choice. You have too much to offer to waste away in the single life. You deserve a man to love you, to raise a family with, and to share your life, share your fears." Sarah stopped when she noticed that Katie was crying. Sarah took her friend into a hug and whispered to her that it would be okay.

"Sweetie, I'm sorry that I made you cry, let's change topics, and go get some dinner. I'm on my own tonight, and thought you might want a girl's night with me. What do you say?"

"Don't feel bad; really, it's just that you are right. If I continue in the same way I have been, before I know it, I will be too old for kids, too bitter for real love, and just a plain old spinster. I'm practically a spinster now."

Sarah could not help herself, but to laugh at Katie's comment. Katie looked up with tears running down her face in dismay.

"Katie, if you are the new definition of a spinster, then let me join the team. You are an astounding woman; you have a fantastic career, with an awesome body for any age, and are more beautiful than you ever were when we were younger. Stop being silly and go get dressed. We have a night on the town ahead of us."

Katie put on a smile and got up to get dressed.

They were in the car within minutes and headed for a local sports bar called, Shooters. It was a great place to go for a casual night out with a friend. They were both in jeans, t-shirts, and ready to hang out and have a few beers. Katie did not usually like beer, but every once in a while it sounded just right.

When they got to the sports bar, it was just getting crowded, so they staked out a table and ordered their first beer, while looking at the menu.

"So, where are the kids tonight?" Katie had forgotten to ask earlier.

"Well, apparently I deserve a night off, so the husband took the kids to a movie, and then they are going to get pizza, at that jungle gym of a pizza place, on Vine Street. I thought about calling you first, but then decided that it would be more fun to just show up on your doorstep."

"That was nice of Tom to take the kids for the night. What a lucky break for me, as well. I have no idea what I would be doing tonight, but I'm sure it would have been unhealthy and heavy in self-loathing, so thank you for saving me." She said with her first real smile of the night.

"You are more than welcome for the save, just promise you'll return the favor someday."

"Anytime you need a save, I'll make sure to show up on your doorstep." They both smiled at one another. Katie realized that it felt good to discover that not everything went back to the way it was, but sometimes it actually got better. The thought struck her like lightening, maybe that applied to Chris, as well. Maybe it did not have to be the same as it was before;

maybe it could be better than that. Maybe all she had to do was reach out the way she had to Sarah and she would find that things were better. It was a thought that she had to push away for a while, because she was not ready to deal with the implications.

Sarah and Katie ate more appetizers, than considered ladylike, and after two beers, they both stopped and switched to soda to avoid a bad night. Katie never drove while intoxicated, that was never an option. They laughed and talked about work, sex, kids, and family.

"Okay, so tell me exactly how long has it been since you had a good man?" Sarah was getting bolder as the night progressed.

"Ugh, I haven't had any good men lately and the last time I had one, at all, was more than a year ago. How embarrassing is that to admit?"

"You have to be kidding me. A woman who looks like you can't possibly have a problem getting a man into bed, so what gives?"

"Well, since you asked so nicely," she replied, "the last man I dated was someone at work. We didn't work together per se, but we were both in the D.A.'s office. He was handsome, extremely successful, and about five years older. It was not really love for either one of us, it was more of a social thing. People seemed to think we fit together and for a while, we were fooled into thinking so too.

It turned out we didn't even like each other that much. He thought I would change and become less independent. In his mind, we would end up married and I would take on the role of the doting wife to a future DA, Senator, etc. He expected me to throw parties, look pretty, and give up my law ambitions. It was impressive to have a wife that was smart but gave up her career to be a mother. He was looking for someone to mold into a political wife.

When he realized that was not going to happen, he stopped being interested. We kept up the façade for months too long and finally I came home to a note that said it was over, his stuff was gone, and he left me my spare key. I was so relieved that I laughed and celebrated with a bottle of champagne. We did become friends again, but it took some time. Everyone thought we were "perfect" for each other, so we didn't ever bother to explain what happened to our friends.

I think he's engaged to a socialite with a degree from a prestigious catholic college, in Boston. Apparently, her idea of being successful was to marry well; which is exactly what Richard wanted. It all worked out for the best. That was my last serious relationship."

"That's quite a dry spell kiddo!" Sarah said with a smile.

"Thanks for pointing that out to me, I hadn't noticed that it's been a while. You're sort of a bitch, as an adult."

"Maybe you should just go sleep with Chris to get it out of your system and not be in a relationship. Then you'd get some sex, which I imagine would be mighty good, and he'd get to have a little piece of you. Seems like a win-win to me."

Katie was not sure if she was serious, but she did have a little smirk on her face, so she was probably teasing.

"That would be fun I'm sure, but I think Chris is looking for a bit more from me than a roll in the hay. I'd hate to have to break his heart."

Both women laughed, but Katie stopped mid chuckle when her eyes glanced towards the front door.

Sarah looked in the same direction to see what caught Katie's eye. Standing at the front door looking absolutely gorgeous, was Chris. He was wearing a green polo shirt that made his eyes gleam, freshly shaven, hair perfectly coiffed. He was a serious hunk. He was standing with a group of men who looked shabby in comparison, and Katie's first thought was that she wanted to touch him. Chris stopped in his tracks when he saw Katie. For a moment, he smiled at her and then looked down and away.

His presence caused Katie's whole body to heat up and go still. It seemed like the room went quiet, but soon Chris and his friends were all at the counter ordering their grub and beer. His back was to them and Katie's heart rate finally settled down. For the first time in at least a minute, she exhaled.

"Why don't you tell me the truth, Katie, it's not Chris you're worried about, it's you. It's your heart that might get broken and that's why you won't let him near you. It is possible, Katie, that this time he'll be different. I think we have both changed a lot in the last ten years, at least I hope so, and I think Chris has changed as well. He's a man now and that makes a difference. Why don't you give him a chance? You want to. I can see it in your eyes when you look at him. You still love him; if you admit it to yourself then maybe you could see a future."

Katie was silent and sat staring at her empty plate. When she looked up there was a tear on her cheek.

"I'm so sorry sweetie; I didn't mean to make you cry again," Sarah said, "Do we need to get out of here?" Katie simply shook her head yes and started to stand up from her stool.

The two women were out the door and the fresh air felt like heaven on her warm face. Katie's face always got red and warm when she cried. They were at the car when Chris called her name. She tried to pretend she did not hear him, but it did not work.

"Katie, please stop, don't act like you don't hear me. Katie?"

Chris spoke her name as if it were a question. She turned to acknowledge him and he smiled at her just a little.

"Thank you for turning around," he spoke softly, "I don't want to be avoided all the time. When I came in you were laughing and you looked so beautiful with a smile on your face. It was nice to be able to see that, since you always frown when I enter a room. I wanted to smile at you and say hello, but your face looked so sad to see me, that I couldn't even bear to look at you."

"I'm sorry Chris, I don't mean to look sad or frown when you are around. I'll be honest, when it comes to you my feelings are so confused that I don't know what to do when I see you. Look, I appreciate you coming out to talk to me, but you should get back to your friends and Sarah and I need to get home. So, I'll see you around, okay? Next time I'll try harder to make it friendly. I don't want things to be difficult for us either. Have a good night."

Katie didn't give him the opportunity to respond she just opened the car door and got in. She even made sure not to look in his direction as they pulled out of the parking spot and left. Katie could see him in the side mirror just watching them leave. Hands in his pockets, shoulders down, he looked so despondent it made her feel awful. Clearly, he was closer to her heart than it appeared.

"You know he watched us until I couldn't see him in the rear view mirror anymore," Sarah advised Katie.

"I don't know what you want me to do, Sarah. It just won't work and he has to know that. I can't help it if it takes him a while to figure it out. Just let it go. We were having such a good night. Let's forget about Chris and go see a movie or something." Sarah agreed.

They spent the rest of the night at Katie's house, drinking wine, and watching chick flick rentals. They laughed and cried at both movies and had a good time just being friends. Katie had forgotten what it was like to have girlfriends; it had been so long since she had invested in anyone but herself. It was late and Sarah called home to say she would be staying the night. She didn't feel drunk, but wine always hit her hard and no one wanted it to hit her on the way home.

The kids were fine and Sarah said Tom preferred she stay than drive, as well. Katie showed Sarah to the guest room, previously used only by Chris, and gave her some pajamas for the night. They were both exhausted from the events and the wine.

When Katie went to check on Sarah, and make sure she was comfortable, Sarah was out like a light. She must have fallen asleep the moment her head hit the pillow. It took a bit longer for Katie. She could not get her mind to stop churning, it was a problem she often had, especially when she was younger. She used to worry all the time and the more she worried the less she slept. She kept thinking about what Sarah said, that maybe it could be different if she gave Chris another shot.

It occurred to her that maybe what she was really worried about was her ability to sustain a relationship. That maybe she would not be enough or that she would screw things up with Chris. To be fair, she was a different person; it was only fair to assume that he could be different, better, as well. She fell asleep with his face on her mind. Thinking about how handsome he had turned out to be. Sunday when she woke up she didn't feel as conflicted as usual.

Sarah was up and gone when Katie woke up, but had left a note saying that she wanted to be home before the kids woke, so they wouldn't think anything was wrong. Katie sometimes wished she had someone to be accountable to, but it didn't matter to anyone how late she slept in, or even where she slept.

Funny how the freedom she always enjoyed somehow made her a little sad and envious this morning. Not someone to dwell on such thoughts, she took her vitamins, had a piece of cantaloupe, and went for a run. She always felt refreshed after a jog in the morning. It was the only time she ever got exercise; anything else was too much work.

She spent the remainder of the day cleaning the house and watching old movies on cable TV. Sundays were usually workdays, but she decided to take this one off and just relax. Her Mom called just before dinnertime and they chatted for a while about nothing in particular. It was a quiet night, and she was in bed with a new book by ten o'clock.

Chapter Twelve

*M*ondays were always hectic because crime went up on the weekends, although the crime in Pennsville differed drastically from that in Boston. Even so, it all had to be reported on Monday and discussed to determine if they were going to prosecute. By the time Katie had a moment to breathe, it was one o'clock, and she was starving.

She and Paul went to the deli within the county office, for a sandwich. There was plenty to discuss, because their child molestation case started back up the next day. The defense had asked for some time to try to find a witness, so the judge gave them the weekend and Monday for the task. It was a stall tactic and everyone knew it, but it was the judge's job to be fair, so he allowed them an extra day for finding the witness.

When they sat down, Katie started to give Paul her ideas for the next round. She noticed Paul not really paying much attention.

"So, what do you think, Paul?" Katie felt that she had rambled on and on about her idea for the case. She did that around him sometimes, still anxious that she needed to prove herself.

"What? Oh, I'm sorry, Katie I was off in thought there for a bit. What did you want to do about the witnesses tomorrow?"

"I'll try not to be offended by your lack of interest in my plan," Katie said with a smile, "I was thinking that instead of trying to attack the witness personally, or discrediting them in any way, I'd like to make them admit that they don't really know what sort of things happened behind closed doors.

I'd like to ask them if they would tell people if they molested children. Would they hide it in every way possible and lie to their own friends if they were molesters? I want to get them to admit that if they were in the same position, as the defendant, they would lie to keep their own secret. That way it keeps the negative focus on the defendant and it doesn't look like I'm tarnishing the character of the witness. What do you think?" she asked.

"I think it's a great plan. This way you still look like a decent human being; which is highly important, and we make the defendant look like the bad guy, not the witnesses who still believe in him. I did notice that the defense couldn't find very many people who still believe in his innocence. That should bode well for our case too.

We have so many people who always thought he was suspicious, or actually saw inappropriate things, I think the jury seemed to be on our side from the word go. I'll never admit that I said this, but you are one hell of a prosecutor, for a kid just out of the gate."

Katie smiled at the compliment and swore that she would never tell a soul he had said such things or ask him to repeat it in the future. They finished their lunch with a bunch of small talk regarding his golf game and Katie's Mom. She really enjoyed working with Paul, he was an amazing mentor.

The week went by and Katie's strategy in the courtroom was going well. She managed to get all of the defenses witnesses to admit, that if they were the defendant they would hide it from everyone. She told the witnesses that it was not their fault, how could they know? She mentioned that it was reasonably possible, that the defendant had just been good at hiding it from them. She told them no one blamed them for not knowing. Eventually, they all agreed with her. They all seemed to open up, and state, that it was possible it had happened. It was perfect, they just wanted to be absolved of any guilt, and then they were free to admit that it was a possibility. That was all she needed to get a conviction.

The defendant was not going to testify on his behalf. Paul and Katie would have preferred that he did, because they knew he had a temper, and it would have looked good for them to have him enraged. A defendant that was angry, rather than one that calmly denied any wrongdoing, always put off jury members. The week was over and she was through every witness the defense had, except the psychologists.

There were two testifying, one for the defense, one "neutral" doctor paid for by the state, and she had a third in case she needed a backup or a rebuttal. Katie was hoping not to need the rebuttal, but at least she had him just in case. The defenses psychologist's reports were very basic and didn't commit him to a definite answer. The defense's doctor was not willing to testify that Riley showed significant signs associated with child molesters, but he did agree that Riley was a candidate for continued mental treatment. Both mental professionals classified him as depressed and anger driven, but not classically defined as a molester. Katie was not sure what to do to win the argument over a classically defined molester. She was hopeful, that if she worked on it over the weekend, she would figure out something. Katie and Paul scheduled a seven in the morning meeting, for Monday, to go over her strategy.

The weekend went quickly, because she spent most of Saturday and Sunday going over her questions and possible answers to have ready for anything the defense could throw at her and Paul. It was a tedious battle of trying to guess what someone might say, and being ready no matter what. Saturday night she did manage to get out of the house long enough to have dinner with Sarah and her family.

The whole family, including Sarah's mother and brothers, were invited and it was a great dinner. The only tough moment was when Darren mentioned that Chris had been in a bad mood for weeks, until one of the kids had asked him if he was menstruating. Apparently he laughed until the kids thought he was going to puke and immediately was back to being his jovial self around the team, and at school in general.

Katie was hoping he would not even be mentioned, but she was happy to hear that he snapped out of his mood. Sarah looked at Katie when Darren first said his name; but she just smiled and looked down at her food. Darren said rumor was that the Coach had a broken heart, but no one knew if that was true or not. Katie just kept eating and didn't make a comment until they changed topics.

Other than a few uncomfortable moments, she had a nice time and was again exhausted when she got home. She went straight to bed and for a change did not have trouble falling asleep. She did have vivid dreams of Chris.

She was in the shower and suddenly she felt a hand on her hip moving her over just a little to the right. She didn't jump because she knew who it was, she would know that touch anywhere. Chris stepped into the shower and she was completely in awe of his body. It was clearly well taken care of and he was still in athlete shape. Broad shoulders, toned arms, and muscular forearms. He was well made and yummy.

She was afraid she might have actually licked her lips when she started checking out his form, but surely, he would not mind. She placed her hand on his shoulder, started to trace his muscles down his arms, then moved to his collarbone, and then down his chest. She caught him smiling out of the corner of her eye. He started to say something, but she shook her head at him and said, "No talking."

With both hands, she began to explore the rest of his body. Her hands and fingers gently running along his chest, he felt firm and strong to her touch, each nipple perking up a little, as she perused his torso. Her hands were now following the small trail of hair down his belly in the valley that existed between his abdominal muscles.

They both understood where she was going. She was aware of him growing against her abdomen with each caress, even though she was pretending not to notice. She went down to his hips and ran her hands along his hipbone and down each side of his thighs. He felt amazing beneath her hands. She could only imagine how good he would feel if she wrapped herself around him, naked, and wet. When her arm brushed his shaft, he took a deep breath and moaned her name.

In that moment, she lost all her willpower and found herself in his arms. They were both wet and the feel of warm drenched skin against skin was intoxicating. First Chris just pulled her against him and kissed gently all over her face. She could feel him hard against her soft belly. His gentle kisses came to rest on her lips and then it became a whirlwind of touch and sensation, and at some point she ended up against the shower wall; her back facing Chris, legs spread.

Chris was washing her with soapy bare hands. His fingertips went up one leg and then down the other, massaging her muscles along the way. He grabbed her backside and squeezed just a little. Then he turned her around, and again with soapy hands washed every little bit of her. He made sure that even the smallest piece of her skin was not missed. When he reached her breasts his fingers twirled each nipple ever so gently, which made her think she might lose it right then and there.

Nevertheless, she held on, she did not want this to stop. Finally, his hand slid down her side, to her hips, then to her warm center, where every stroke made her knees weaker, her body shudder, and before long, she was calling Chris' name and wilting in his arms.

As a result Katie was, after her wild dream, wide awake at two in the morning going over court documents and drinking her third cup of coffee. The only good thing about being up was that she was getting somewhere with the psychological review files. She was certain that she had found a loophole that would allow her to get the defense's psychologist to agree with her and say that the defendant was a danger to people. It was a long shot, but she would keep working with it and see if Paul had any ideas on Monday morning. She spent a few more hours poring over the reports and finally felt sleepy. She lay down for about forty-five minutes and begrudgingly gave up on sleep, so she got up for her morning run.

She was still tired, so she didn't do her full run, but it felt good to be sweaty and out of breath. Since she had done so much work in the middle of the night, she had the whole day to do with, as she liked. She decided to do a little shopping in the downtown center. It was fairly small, but she just wanted to browse anyway. She would stop at Martha's for ice cream and enjoy the warm day. It was such a gorgeous day, the sun shining bright and blue skies, so she shopped first. She picked up a few knickknacks at one of the local antique shops and a new summer dress, at a trendy shop that was new to Pennsville.

When Katie got to Martha's there was a small line, but it gave her time to decide which ice cream she would choose. She always looked around at each choice, and usually asked to taste the weekly flavor, but always ended up with the same thing, a mint chip, strawberry and chocolate banana split with all the fixings. The place had not changed much since she was a kid. The floor was still the same black and white tile, and the wood shelves behind the ice cream freezers were filled with candy jars, and teddy bears.

The smell, oh, the sweet smell of waffle cones, they got her every time. Katie rarely ordered one, but she loved the scent whirling around her. It always instantly relaxed her, odd but true. Martha's grin grew wider when she saw Katie in line. When she made it to the front, they had a little time to chat since she was the last unattended costumer in the shop. Martha asked about work, which seemed like a safe topic.

"I'm working a tough case at the moment, but it's good. I feel great about the opportunity I have here, so I'm still glad I made the move. How's business?"

"Business has been the same forever. I'm still waiting for the day someone walks in and offers to buy the place. Then I'll go to the Bahamas for a few weeks and retire in peace. Of course, give me two months or less and I'll be so bored I'll probably have to get a job." Katie smiled and laughed as was appropriate. Martha, it was known throughout town, had been offered a lot of money on more than one occasion for the ice cream parlor and refused. No one bothered to ask anymore because it was obvious she loved the place. Martha was there every day from open to close and only had help on the weekend evenings, so that the crowds did not have to wait that long. Martha was a creature of habit and everyone knew she would never sell the place willingly.

"Well Martha, give me a few more years to save up and I'll buy this place from you for sure."

"You got it, I won't be taking any offers without consulting you first." They both grinned at one another. When Martha handed over the massive banana split, the last patron was leaving and they were officially alone. Katie sat down at a table, near the window, and started in on her ice cream dream.

"So, Chris Staller was in here a few weekends ago looking for you. It seemed really important. Did he manage to find you?"

"Ah, yeah… ummm, he actually was able to find me that day. Thanks for letting him know where I was. It wasn't super important, but thanks for the help anyway."

"It sure seemed important to him at the time, but I'm glad he found you no matter what the reason."

They both knew that Katie was trying to down play the situation, but Martha did not seem willing to push for more information about what he needed with her that day.

"I still remember when you two were in here all the time for ice cream. What a handsome couple the two of you made. He was so shy and reserved until he started dating you, and then he turned into a handsome, charismatic young man. All the girls were gaga over him, but he never looked at any of them the way he looked at you. You know, if I remember correctly, when you left town he pretty much stopped dating altogether. It was so sad to see him so lonely."

"I'm sure he went on a few dates after I left town. He was a popular guy when I left and I'm sure he was not lacking for attention, from the senior girls. Don't feel too sorry for him, Martha." Katie was hoping that would end the conversation, but she should have known better.

"Oh, honey, I never said the girls didn't try, I just said that he didn't date. He was in here most weekend nights, working with me. We would chat about school and his plans for college. He was always polite to the girls when they came in, but he never went out with them. I'll tell you one thing he sure was good for business. I had every girl in town here for ice cream on the weekends.

He talked about you some, when he first started working here, but after a while, he stopped and I never bugged him. He never gave up hope that you would call or write. He was a good kid, a good worker, and seemed content to be here while the other kids were partying. I do love that boy, as if he were mine. Being around Chris always made me wish I had kids of my own. He has always done an excellent job of making me feel important to him, which was, is, sweet. He even used to call me from college to check in, so in a way I guess I do have a son like him. Hopefully someday he'll find someone else who thinks he's as wonderful as I do, someone to love him, forever."

They both fell silent. Katie hadn't realized that Chris was so close to Martha. That explained why she had been so willing to offer Katie's whereabouts, a few weeks ago. She knew that when he got to college Chris changed, because he had said so, but that was a year later, and a person cannot be expected to wait forever.

She finished her banana split, without speaking much to Martha, except to thank her and telling her good bye.

For the rest of the day she tried not to think about Chris, Martha, or anything unpleasant. She headed home and on a whim stopped at the pet store to look around. She had been thinking of getting a dog for protection, but when she left the store, she had a new kitten and all the supplies. So much for an attack dog. The tabby was gray, black, and white with flashing green eyes.

She fell in love the moment the little gal meowed. It was a little girl according to the store clerk, and she was fully vaccinated, and had been spayed. Katie wasn't sure what to call her yet, but knew it would come to her as soon as the kitty showed some more personality. The cat managed to brighten up her whole day and Katie soon forgot all about Chris. Katie and the kitten played with all of the toys she bought and ate dinner together. Katie even let the kitty sleep under the covers where it was cozy. It was somewhat nice to have a warm little body next to her all night. For such a small animal, the new cat put off a lot of heat. For a change, Katie did not feel so lonely.

Chapter Thirteen

*K*atie over slept, thanks to a night of cuddling with her warm little tabby, who went right back to sleep, even before she left for work. Not exactly the best way to start a new week, but the meeting with Paul went well, despite her tardiness. They both had the same idea from their reading over the weekend, and as they talked it over, it became a decisive plan. They were confident with the case up to this point, but with juries, it was often hard to tell.

Luckily, the defendant's psychologist was not willing to rule out the fact that he was a child molester; he just stated that the classical signs of being one were not present. Therefore, Katie was going to play up the fact that they could not rule it out and then have her witness, as a rebuttal, to confirm that in recent years most psychologists subscribed to the idea that there was no classical definition for a child molester. If it went as she expected, the other psychologist would look non-committal and out of date. It sounded easy, but she knew it would be a challenge.

Katie and Paul sat quietly during a two-hour question and answer session with the state facility psychologist. The lead defense attorney kept asking the same question in a different way and even the judge looked bored. When it was Katie's turn, she felt confident and sure of herself. The jury seemed completely on her side and it was plain to see that they responded to her line of questioning more so than the defense. It went better than expected and Paul was extremely pleased with her performance in the courtroom.

"Katie," Paul said as they walked into his office after their day in court, "you were spectacular. I think we played them perfectly today and the jury is obviously responding to you very nicely. I am positive that we will have our man this time."

"It was a good day, but let's not count this as a win yet. Tomorrow let's meet before the trial again and go over the next doctor's testimony. There is a good chance that they will change their tactic and we need to be ready to change ours, as well."

"Okay, okay, we'll meet tomorrow and I'll try and be less positive, Miss Negative." Paul said with a smile and laughed when Katie let her natural urge to stick her tongue out at him win, over her usually reasonable, sort of stuffy, behavior.

"I'm leaving your office now before I do anything else childish and inappropriate for the work place." Katie said.

"Don't take yourself or life so seriously, Katie. It's good to have fun every now and then. Now, go find something special to do to celebrate your success."

"Say hello to Helene for me. I'll see you in the morning, funny man." She grinned at him one more time and stepped out of his office.

She spent a few more hours at work before taking off and heading home. Her Mom and Sarah had both called her, but she didn't feel like chatting. She was nervous about the trial the next day and just wanted to relax and be alone. She was sitting on the couch reading when someone knocked on the door. She wasn't expecting anyone and it was late, so she made sure to check her peephole before opening the door. No one was there when she looked outside, so with extra care she opened the door. She looked around the porch first and saw no one, on the street and the only evidence that someone had been there was another bouquet of flowers.

This time they were white and she wondered if they were meant as a truce. They were just as lovely as the others were, and smelled magnificent. He really was a persistent man. When she last saw him, she told him it would never happen, but she was angry then. She knew she should at least consider the idea now that she wasn't so upset. Her whole life was about reason; she should probably apply some of it to her personal relationships.

She fell asleep on the couch, her new flowers in a vase close by, and the tiara she had yet to return, atop her head. All the while Olivia was purring on her lap. They woke up around midnight and finally made it to their bed. As she passed the kitchen, she placed the flowers on the table, made a mental note to call Chris, and say thank you. She thought it was also time to extend her own olive branch. It was ridiculous that after all these years they could not be friends. She had thought maybe even more after her weekend away, but that just seemed even more impossible now. Certainly, friends they could do, she would do something about that as soon as possible.

The next day she couldn't seem to get herself going for work, even after two cups of coffee she was still dragging. By the time she got to Paul's office she was fifteen minutes late.

"I praise you for a job well done and you take that to mean that you can slack off today?" He was only kidding, but Katie felt bad about being late anyways.

"You know that I'm usually very punctual. I just couldn't get started this morning. So, before you tease me anymore, let's just get to work, old man." He looked up with a feigned look of shock and then at a chair for her to sit and get to work.

They spent an hour going over possible scenarios and finally had to head to the courtroom. Unfortunately, the day started badly and only got worse. The defense had regrouped and had a new approach and a second psychiatrist, Dr. Michaels. He had been on the witness list for some time, but was not expected to testify. This time they were quicker to the point, and did a much better job of making it seem like the defendant might not be harmful. It only took a reasonable doubt to keep someone out of prison. This doctor had also spent time with the victims and actually said that their stories were all so similar, that it was possible that they were in cahoots. He actually used the phrase, 'in cahoots'.

Katie and Paul were way ahead of the game before Dr. Michael's testimony, but agreed they needed to make up some ground after him. Katie did her best to try to make it swing back in their favor, but the jury was not responding as well as usual. She wasn't sure if she was off her game or if they were just in a different mood.

The next two days they worked to combat the doubt that the defense was building into their case. They still had their rebuttal psychiatrist, and that would be the last witness for the whole trial, so Katie and Paul worked very hard to get ready for his testimony. Fortunately, he was a seasoned expert witness and they expected him to do well for them. They spent most of Thursday night with Doctor Shultz preparing for every angle that the defense could take. When all was said and done, they were pleased with the results.

The next day would be tricky, but Paul said he was confident that they would pull out the victory. Katie got little to no food or sleep most of the week. She went to bed within a half hour of arriving home, in anticipation of a long day in court the next day. As she walked by the kitchen Thursday night, she saw the now wilting roses and again reminded herself that she needed to call Chris and say thank you. At this point, it was almost too late, but she had little choice. She had been going non-stop with work all week and until the verdict came in, she would be busy.

Friday morning turned out to be a beautiful morning. The sky was blue and crisp and the air was just cool enough to need a light jacket. Katie was feeling good about the day and confident about court. All the kids that testified against the defendant were in the courtroom, per her request, so that the jury could see them one more time before heading in to make their decision. She had this case in the bag, she just knew it, and when the defense rested, all that would be left to do was give her closing statement. There was an hour lunch break coming up, so the judge extended it to ninety minutes and let everyone rest up for the closing statements. She was ready to go and found it disappointing that she had to wait to seal the deal.

Being patient was one of the things she didn't do well. Paul and Katie took the teens for a bite of lunch, along with their parents. The kids were quiet, and the parents tried to make small talk, but everyone simply wanted to have the matter settled. As the group was leaving to return to the courtroom, Josh stopped her before she walked away from the table.

"I just wanted to say that I got the feeling that it meant a lot to Coach, that you were the one to talk to me that night we came in to the station. He asked for you specifically and told me there was no one better to help me than you. He said you were the finest person he had ever met. I can see why he feels that way now that I've met you too. I just think you should know he said that about you. He seems to be sad lately, and I guess I just thought that maybe you were the one who could help him again. He's been good to me, so maybe this will return the favor. Either way, thanks for all you have done for the other kids and me. I really think you nailed it today."

Katie was speechless, her eyes watery and her throat felt dry. Luckily, just when Josh was about to leave, she found her voice.

"You're welcome," she said a tad above a whisper, "And thank you, too." Josh nodded and with a boyish smile in her direction, he walked away. He was usually a quiet kid and she was surprised that he had wanted to speak to her at all. She wasn't sure how to feel about what he said, except that she was surprised that Chris seemed to trust her as much as he did. She knew he cared for his kids and was flattered that he thought her a safe place for them. More than that, she was moved by the fact that even before she had made a big stink about his behavior in the past, he admitted to someone else how she had changed his life, that she had made it better.

Obviously, he didn't tell the kids all about her or their history, but she what she read into that statement was that he regretted losing her. Moreover, if he was telling other people and using it to help his students get through rough times, then maybe he really did care about her. She needed to talk to him soon about the flowers and about being friends, and maybe even someday more than friends. There had to be a way to work things out between them. She didn't have much time to think about Chris or to make a phone call because recess was over and she was up first.

"The defense would have you believe that classic child molesters, rapists, and abusers tend to use their own children for sexual pleasure, and that since the defendant did not, he is somehow special. The idea that Mr. Riley is special or somehow less harmful to children because he did not abuse his own children makes me ill. The fact is he did abuse his own children, mentally and physically. His actions eventually isolated them, because they didn't want to bring friends home. He used his children to create opportunity to fulfill his sexual misconduct.

The fact that he never touched his own sons in a sexual manner does not automatically prove that he did not touch others. Let's say I agree that he is not a classic case, it doesn't negate the reality that he did, on at least the occasions we have heard in this courtroom, abuse, molest and, or harm these children." Katie turned and gestured toward the kids who had testified so the jury would really look at the boys, "Is their pain less real, is their unwarranted shame less heart wrenching? I don't think so. I don't believe you think so.

By using his sons in this manner, he did harm him. His oldest son shared with all of us, through testimony, how the behavior his father exhibited has affected his life. He testified about his fear of marriage, of love, of family, and most of all his hesitation to have children. His son admitted that he was never touched sexually, but that he was aware of his father's behavior. His son was beaten regularly when his Dad was frustrated and had not had a sexual release in a while. He never saw his father with a woman, other than the few years before his mother left. He admits to driving friends away for their own good. He shared with us his pain and loneliness as a child, and now a young adult, without friends. Abuse is still abuse, and his son is forever scarred by his youth.

Then there are the boys that he did molest and rape. The boys who were taught to fear people, fear men, and to mistrust themselves, all thanks to a man who was in a position of authority in their lives. He may not have been their parent, their teacher, or their religious guide, but he was a parent. In your youth, when you were at someone's house, you listened to their parents and followed the rules. He was a grown up and therefore must know what was right and wrong. That is what we teach our children and expect from them. In this case, the lesson does not apply because he was not in the right, he was wrong.

By no stretch of the imagination was his behavior appropriate, acceptable, or within the lines of the law. He is a criminal against children, his own and ours. He is a man for whom we should feel no sympathy, we must make him pay for what he has done to the boys sitting in the courtroom today. Let us not forget that these are only the few that we know about. How many other kids did he steal innocence from, here in our county or others? How many childhoods has he ruined with his sexually predatory behavior?

Take this opportunity to prove to these victims that right prevails over wrong, and good always wins the battle against evil. Mr. Riley is a cold hearted, child abuser, child molester, and child rapist. Let us not forget that and let *him* not forget that we will not stand by and let his crimes go unpunished in our town, in our lives. Thank you and God bless."

The defense did the best they could to remind the jury that any doubt in their minds, was reasonable doubt. Moreover, reasonable doubt must mean acquittal on all charges. Katie was not moved by the defense's closing and she didn't think the jury would be either, at least she hoped not. She was happy that they decided not to stand up and call the teen's liars again, perhaps because they were all sitting in the courtroom with their parents. Not to mention that after Katie's closing several of the boys, and their parents were crying. It made tough work for the defense.

The jury took only forty-five minutes to deliberate. When they returned Katie knew, by the look that some of them gave her, that the verdict was guilty. They made eye contact, and that was one of the first things taught about juries in school, if they do not look you in the eye, then they did not go your way.

The foreperson read the verdict and with a proud voice declared the jury to have found Mr. Riley guilty on all counts of molestation, child endangerment, rape, and abuse charges. The crowd there to witness the trial cheered and Paul and Katie were ecstatic to have won. She received many pats on the back, words of congratulations from the spectators, and words of gratitude from the parents. It had been a long battle and no one had suffered the way the children had, which made it the sweetest of all victories. The kids thanked Katie and Paul, with hugs, and then were off to celebrate with their parents.

Katie sat in the courtroom long after everyone else was gone. Paul had hoped for an early verdict so he could take Helene out for dinner. It was their anniversary, and this night he was ecstatic to have two reasons to celebrate. Paul was thrilled with her work, mentioned that if she kept it up soon she would be running the show, and would not have him looking over her shoulder in court anymore. Of course, she did not feel that he was a babysitter, but he was definitely in charge. She was lucky she had been allowed to run the whole trial. Most fledglings would have been permitted to say very little or nothing at all. This was the role she was initially to have played, until Paul saw her pretrial and jury selection work.

Now, she was on her way and all she had to do was keep it up, which she immediately realized was a lot of pressure. As she sat in the courtroom, she could not help but feel overwhelmed. The reality that the better you are, the more that people expect from you, set in and she felt gratified and scared.

For some reason it reminded her that she had no one to go home to, no one with whom to share her victory, or her fears. She could call her Mom or Sarah, but it was not the same. She wanted someone who was her own, who would know the moment she walked in the door that she needed a hug or needed to vent. She felt the lacking more in this moment than she had in years. She was usually good at convincing herself it was not a bad thing to be on her own and independent.

Dependency was not part of who she was normally, it was not a weakness she allowed herself to possess. She was not needy, but all of a sudden she needed someone and the only person who came to mind, was Chris.

Chapter Fourteen

When Katie walked through her front door, she had completely lost the high from the win in the courtroom. Her mind was mush and all she could hope for was a long bath, and a few hours with a good book, and some sleep. Her message machine was flashing, but she didn't feel up to returning calls. She let the messages wait and started bath water instead. After a long soak, she snuggled into her pajamas, with a glass of merlot, and a book in her hand.

Her phone rang and again she decided to let it go. She was not in the mood for congratulations, even though they would be appreciated. It would be hard to convince anyone she was thrilled when she actually felt sad. Less than two minutes later the phone rang again and this time she figured she had better just answer the damn phone. She had a feeling it wouldn't stop until she did anyway.

"Hello?"

"Katie, oh my gosh, I'm so glad you answered. I have tried you at home and then at the office. I already left you one message, but I was calling to leave one last message before I had to go to bed. Are you okay, where have you been?"

"I have been home since the end of the trial, but not in the mood to talk. It's sort of an emotional overload at this point. I'm sorry that I seem to have scared you, is everything okay? Is something wrong with the kids?"

"No, no the kids are fine. I just wanted you to know, and well, I thought you would want to know, that Chris has been in an accident."

Katie's heart stopped for just a second and she suddenly found it hard to breathe. It could not be true, it hurt too much to think of the possibility.

"I don't know exactly what happened," Sarah went on, "but I do know that he was taken to the hospital. The ambulance went to the high school and the kids were apparently pretty freaked out by the whole event. I know you refuse to admit that you are head over heels for the man, but something told me that you would want to know. Did I do the right thing?"

"Um…yes, yes, of course I want to know. Thank you for calling me."

"You're welc… " Katie hung up the phone without letting Sarah finish. She didn't know exactly what to do, but she knew sitting on the phone was not the answer. She needed to get dressed and head to the hospital. What if he was dying or in surgery? Did he have anyone to be there for him? He had no family, at least none that was close. She couldn't handle the idea of him all alone and possibly scared by whatever happened to him.

Katie was quick to pull on some jeans and a t-shirt, and pull her hair back into a ponytail before she got in the car, and headed to the hospital. There was only one hospital in the county, there were several urgent care centers, but for the size of each small town nearby, they only needed one hospital. She drove faster than was her normal tendency, and could barely find the control to park her vehicle in a straight line. She ran into the emergency room and asked the first nurse she saw where to find Chris Staller. The nurse pointed her to the information desk.

When she reached the information desk, a nurse asked her if she was next of kin. She knew from past visits to hospitals that information was not given to anyone who was not, so she lied and said she was his sister and was given his room number.

"Is he in ICU?" she asked the nurse.

"No, he is not. I'm sure the patient can explain better than I can what his situation is, as I don't have his chart, only his room assignment." Katie could tell she had over stayed her welcome at the information desk and left without another word, not even a thank you.

Katie hated hospitals. Other than the one time when her mom had gallbladder surgery, she hadn't stepped in one since her father's passing. To her, they smelled like musty bodies, or death with a twinge of sanitizer. The elevator ride up to the third floor took far too long. You would think in a place where life and death were often seconds apart, the damn pulley system they used would work faster than a geriatric patient would. Stepping out into the hallway she felt a little sick to her stomach. Even though the walls, for some god-awful reason, were Pepto-Bismol pink, they were not helping her nausea.

She checked the signs and made a left toward rooms 315-329. As she walked a few feet down the hall, she made a silent prayer that when she opened the door he would not look as bad as her father had, when she last saw him. Bruised, battered, and taking his final breaths.

When she got to the door of room 316, she could hear voices and wondered if she was interrupting a visit by someone else. What if he did have people to be with him? What if Amanda had been called? She did not want to be embarrassed again, but it did sound like male voices, so she decided to take a chance and opened the door. The only light in the room was from the television, which happened to be on one of the sports news channels. What a surprise. It also explained the male voices.

She walked into the room and saw him lying in the bed. His head was completely wrapped in gauze and he was either sound asleep, or unconscious. She assumed that if he had been unconscious he would still be in the ICU, but the idea was scary anyway.

She went to the side of his bed and sat in the chair. He was breathing heavily and she did not see any tubes in his nose or mouth, so he was definitely conscious and simply asleep. She still wasn't sure what was wrong with him, but the head wound must be bad for all that wrapping. She reached her hand out and took a hold of his. He did not stir and she tried not to make a noise, as she sat there for more than an hour, just memorizing his face.

He had more lines that the boy in her memory, of course. He had a few scars that she didn't remember from when he was a young man. She assumed sports were to blame for most of them. It was funny on men; scars seemed only to add to their appeal. They made him look manly and tough. They actually made him more attractive. As if, she needed more reasons.

She fell asleep with her head on the hospital bed still holding on to Chris' hand. She would have slept all night had she not felt his hand move, which jolted her back to reality, to a hospital room, where Chris was hurt and she had no clue what was wrong. Katie woke to the feel of something soft and a little wet against her forehead, like lips. She opened her eyes and looked up into his.

"Good morning, beautiful, or is it good evening?" Chris whispered. "How did you know I was here?"

Katie jumped up to a sitting position, back completely straight as she tried to gain some composure.

"Oh, Chris, I'm so glad to see you awake and hear your voice. Sarah called me and told me you had an accident at the school, that an ambulance had taken you away, and that the faculty and students were all very upset. I thought you might need someone and I was so afraid that you might be seriously hurt. Are you seriously hurt?"

"Well, I have had worse, and to tell the truth I'm almost a bit embarrassed to tell you what happened. I can't believe you came here, you are actually the last person I expected to see when I woke up to a warm hand in mine."

"We can talk about that in a minute, Chris. What happened to you? Please, tell me you are going to be alright." Chris smiled up at her and she melted. What he must think of her and her wishy-washy attitude about him, she wished she knew what he was thinking.

Chris, looking up at Katie's face, thought she looked so scared, and upset, that it made him want to hold her. He was also a little thrilled to see that she cared. She was clearly scared at the thought that he might be truly hurt. He reached his hand to Katie's face and gently stroked each cheek.

"There is nothing to worry about, my sweet princess; I'm fine, especially now that you are here with me."

Katie gulped and made no reply, so Chris continued.

"I was teaching my last class of the day. We were doing a team building exercise that used a baseball like game to make the kids work together. I wanted every kid to reap the benefit of the game, so I was pitching, and the students were doing the rest. One of my smaller students was up to bat. Every time we play any game, the rest of the class treats him as an automatic out, a failure. I know the problem is confidence and self-esteem, so in my wisdom I pitched him an easy, right over the plate ball that he could not possibly miss.

It worked, the ball made contact instantly and we all heard the famous crack of the bat. The only problem was that he made such quick contact that by the time I saw the ball coming at my head my reflexes were not prepared, and I was hit. Not only was I hit, my fair maiden, but it hit me square in the forehead.

My kids were frantic, of course, and one of them went to get help. I was out for a while, I'm not sure how long, but when I came to my boss was kneeling next to me calling my name. The head is one of the places that bleeds the most when scraped, cut, or scratched. So, there was blood all over me, which did not help the kids or the ambulance person who was there trying to assess me, before bringing me here. I was actually feeling fine, or so I thought, but when I tried to stand up it was impossible. Then the ambulance took me away and brought me here. That is what happened."

"Oh my, is there any brain trauma?"

"Nope."

"Do they think you might need surgery of any kind?"

"Nope."

"Well, something happened to your head, because there is an entire roll of gauze wrapped around your head."

"Oh that, the person who bandaged me has worked in a hospital for all of three days and got a little carried away with the gauze."

Chris was smiling at her in his usual, sweet *surely, you think I am cute*, way.

"So, you mean to tell me that I flew over here because you have a small scratch on your head, which only bled a lot due to its location?"

"Well, since you seem so upset, perhaps this will help, I do have one hell of a bump and a mild concussion. That is why I'm staying here, because there is no one at home to take care of me and make sure I don't slip into a coma. Plus, I'm fairly certain that this splitting headache of mine is never going away."

"The coma factor makes me feel better, but I can't believe I got all upset over a little hit on the noggin."

"I don't know that I would call it little," he said playing offended, "for your information, it really hurt. People were very worried about me for a while there, you know. Obviously, someone thought it was important enough to spread the word down to the middle school and for you to get a call from Sarah."

"I guess it probably seemed scary at the time, but come on, it's not like you required surgery or anything." Now Katie was just playing with him.

"It may not have required surgery, Miss Sympathetic, but it did require several sutures to close my head. It's a damn good thing you chose law school and not med school, you have a horrible bed side manner."

Chris was pouting and Katie busted out a laugh. She almost fell out of her seat she was laughing so hard.

"I'm sorry, did I miss something here?" Chris questioned, "I thought I was in the hospital, overnight for observation, with fear that I might fall into a coma. Did I miss the funny part?" Apparently, he said something even funnier by Katie's reaction.

All that did was make Katie laugh even harder and the next time she was able to control herself there were tears streaking down her face. Chris wanted to act sad or even insulted, but couldn't. His façade broke down and he was laughing just as hard as she had been.

"Don't make me laugh, it hurts too much." He complained and yet they spent the next few minutes trying to compose themselves, but every time one of them stopped laughing, the other would start, and it would just get worse. Finally, a nurse came by and said if they were not quiet, even though she was family, Katie would not be allowed to visit much longer. They both promised to be good and the nurse gave them one last stern look; which almost made them come unglued again as she walked out of the room.

"So, how are we related?" Chris asked with a confused grin.

"I had to tell them we were family or they weren't going to let me in to see you, it was a tiny white lie."

"I didn't know you were a bold faced liar, you learn something new every day." Chris smiled and she looked at him in a way that confused him. "What does that look on your face mean?"

"What look?" Katie questioned.

"Your face changed just now, something happened. Your eyes aren't shining anymore and now you seem...foggy." He sat there and let her just be with his question and waited for her to respond. Hoping when she did she would finally open up about her feelings to him. His mind reading skills were not as good as they used to be, but he sure wished they would kick in soon.

◆◆◆

It bothered Katie that he was paying such close attention. The interruption had spoiled the moment; she could feel the walls rising again. She was disappointed in herself. She wanted to be braver than this, and tougher, less afraid, but she wasn't.

"I'm not sure what foggy looks like on a person Chris, but I'm fine."

"Foggy, murky, gloomy, sad, you know what I meant. What happened?"

"I'm fine Chris; I should probably get going soon though, I'm sure you need some rest."

"Katie, do not do this, talk to me. You came here for a reason. Why did you come here?"

"I thought you were hurt, that's all. I wanted to make sure you were all right. I know that things have been strained between us, but I care about you. Don't make this into something it's not."

"Katie, you are lying again, I know that it means something. I saw your face when you woke up, you were concerned about me, and I know what I saw. Why can't you tell me the truth?"

"Chris, let's not do this now, here, it can wait until…some other time."

Katie stood up and went to reach for her purse when Chris grabbed her arm and pulled her down into an uncomfortable position on the hospital bed.

"Katie, I'm not going to let you walk out of here without talking things out, tell me why you came here tonight."

"You know why I came here, so I don't see why we need to have a long conversation about it, especially while you are holding me in this position; which is not in the least bit comfortable for me."

Chris helped her move a little on the bed, trying to make her more comfortable, but without letting her get away. He released her arm only to grab a hold of her hand.

"I hope I know why you came here, but I don't know anything until you tell me. Tell me Katie, why are you here?"

She was silent and tried to look at anything in the room but Chris. She knew she could muscle her way away from him. Nevertheless, something kept her there. She did not know if she could handle the truth. She knew what it was now, but saying it aloud to Chris was too hard.

"Chris..." she started to protest.

"Katie, look at me when you talk, please. I need to see your face, to read your eyes in order to know what's real."

Katie turned her head to look him straight in the eyes.

"That's better, tell me what you have to say, tell me how you feel."

"Chris, I can't do this right now. It was so hard to come here, not knowing what I would find or whom I would find. Part of me thought I might look foolish barging in here since we have no real ties. What if one of your girlfriends had been here, wouldn't that have been awkward? More importantly, I didn't know what was wrong with you. I was scared. When Sarah called me, I didn't have any details, so it could have been anything. I thought for sure you were unconscious when I walked into the room. The only thing that made me feel better was when they directed me here, rather than ICU. In Boston an ambulance means something, how was I to know an ambulance gets called around here for little scratches?"

Chris smiled just a little and then politely reminded her it was a little more than a scratch. He gave her the "how could you" look, that involved dimples and a half smile.

"That's all I can say Chris. I don't have the words or the courage to say the rest tonight. Can you live with that?"

Chris had been slowly moving to a sitting position in his hospital bed, and was getting closer to Katie. He moved his hand from hers, slowly stroked up her arm, to her shoulder, and finally rested his hand on Katie's face. She closed her eyes at the shear heat of his hand against her skin. She could not bring herself to open her eyes for fear that he would see his effect clearly displayed.

"Katie, please look at me. I won't hurt you; I just want to see you, please." It took her sometime to open her eyes, but when she did, his face was closer than she realized. He seemed to be moving closer with each intake of air and she could feel his warm breath on her face. He smelled like raspberries and she wondered if he tasted like them too.

"Princess," Chris slowly whispered, "I can wait until you are ready to talk to me, about what is so obviously here between us. I will wait, but know that keeping it to yourself does not make it any less true. What we have is real, and no amount of hiding it, will change that. It's a fact, I love you, and Katie, I know that you love me too."

With that, Chris moved the half-inch closer to her lips and gently kissed them, as they quivered from his touch. She was not sure what was happening to her, but her whole body was shaking. It was not as if it was a first kiss or even their first kiss, but she could not help but feel nervous. Something about this one was different. Chris' lips were gentle and warm, never trying to do anything more than caress Katie's. It was Katie who eventually decided the kiss should be more. She moved her arms to encircle his neck and parted his lips with her tongue.

"Hmmm," she moaned, "you taste like them too."

She tasted the warm raspberry flavor of his mouth as they matched each other with ever thrust of their tongues. Chris slowed the kiss down and gently nibbled on her lip. Katie made a deep sound in her throat and Chris knew that she was finally letting go, she was allowing herself to be free with him. He kissed her chin, her cheeks, and then moved to her neck. He had always loved to nibble on her neck. He found each earlobe and gave them a gentle tug before making his way back to her sweet, sweet lips.

"Kiss me Chris, and not like an invalid." Katie begged.

With that challenge thrown down at his bedside, Chris touched her lips with his thumb and found them quaking, she was clearly in need of him. The feel of her soft skin, so sweet and gentle made him swoon a bit. Katie closed her eyes with what he hoped was ecstasy. Their kisses were pure and satisfying. He passed his thumb over her top lip, the fuller of the two, and then ran it across her lower one. Katie's mouth seemed to shiver even more.

Chris brushed his tongue along the bottom lip and gave it a tug with his teeth, then moved to her upper lip with the same erotic treatment. Soon, her whole body was in a state of tremors. Chris wrapped her in his arms, at the same moment that he took possession of her mouth.

The minute he covered her mouth with his she simply folded into his arms. It was passion, jealousy, anger, and fear all mixed into one fierce kiss. Their kiss was like experiencing a fireball of heat that scorched their mouths, but somehow felt too good to stop. It was the kind of kiss that girls dream about when they are first in love, like in the movies. The kind that makes your knees buckle. Thank goodness she was lying down.

Her body was in shock and very still, but her heart was beating so fast she could hear it. On the other hand, maybe that was Chris' heart. Who could tell? She moved his left hand to cup one of her breasts, just as she had done so many years ago when they were kids, and he would not touch her without permission. The moment was taking a turn to the R rated when a voice interrupted them.

"Visiting hours are ov...er," advised a very surprised nurse as she opened the door, "I'm so sorry to have interrupted. Um… you'll have to come by and visit your brother tomorrow, I'm afraid." Then in total shock and with a bit of horror on her face, the nurse left the room.

Katie looked at Chris and they both broke out in laughter, oh what the poor nurse must have been thinking.

"My sister, huh?" Chris was the first to speak.

"I hadn't planned on getting caught necking in your hospital bed."

"Is that what we were doing, necking? Funny, I don't remember you ever calling it that, even when we were kids. This is classic, I might have some explaining to do around here once word gets out around town, we might be a town away but this will surely make the rounds of gossip. Luckily, everyone who knows me, knows I don't have a sister."

Chris went to brush aside a strand of hair from her forehead and Katie flinched from his touch.

"I need to go now, but I'll call you soon and check in on your condition. It's late and I have case files to wrap up tomorrow."

"That's right, the Riley verdict was expected today, and do I need to ask how it went?"

"The State was victorious and Riley will be sentenced in three days for his crimes against children. We got lucky."

"Something tells me it had nothing to do with luck and everything to do with you." Katie did not speak, but she did not leave either. "Don't let this be the end, Katie. Tell me that when you walk out, it won't be as if this night never happened. Tell me we won't be starting over. Please, say something." She wouldn't look at him.

"I'll call you tomorrow," was her reply and then she got up, grabbed her purse, and walked out of the door. Chris could do nothing but sigh and rest his head on his pillow. He was actually having a hard time holding his head up, but when they were kissing, the pain was worth the trouble. Now, his head felt like an orchestra had taken up residence. Chris closed his eyes and didn't sleep for hours; he simply laid there, thinking of Katie, and what he would do to win her heart

Chapter Fifteen

*K*atie drove home much slower than she had when heading to the hospital. There were so many thoughts running through her mind that she felt lost. She didn't know what to do next or what she wanted for sure. Her lips still felt warm from his kisses and her mouth still tasted of raspberries.

By the time she got home, she was exhausted. Between the elation of winning her first case in Pennsville, to thinking that Chris was seriously hurt, to feeling sexy and lustful for him, and then back to confused and scared, it was a lot to feel for one day. Why was she so afraid? She wasn't sure why this one thing, this one man, made her a coward. She was tired of running from her feelings and from Chris. If she was going to stay in this town, she needed to deal with him, which meant that she needed to deal with herself.

If only she knew how to do that. She wanted to feel the way she did in Chris' arms, all the time. She was never going to have it with anyone if she didn't just take the leap. Isn't that what Sarah had been telling her all this time? To try, to go for it, let herself love, and be loved. The reality was, even if it did not work out; she already knew she could take care of herself. She didn't need it but she really, really wanted it! And, not just in her dreams.

There was no sleep for Katie until it was almost morning, when she finally was exhausted enough to crash. When the doorbell rang and woke her up, she was not pleased. She looked at the clock; it was only six thirty in the morning. It was a Saturday and she was planning to go into the office, but even then, she wasn't due to wake up for at least another sixty minutes. It was an hour that she truly needed. Her plan was to ignore the damn bell. It rang two more times, so she yelled as loud as she could "Go away!"

The only problem with the plan was that the doorbell kept ringing. She finally gave in and with a groan got out of bed, and headed for the front door. She didn't even bother to look in the mirror on the way out of her bedroom. At this time of the morning, whoever was bothering her, deserved to see her in full morning glory. Then, maybe they would understand and appreciate that they had disrupted her sleep. She swung the door open violently.

"This better be important," she demanded and as the last words left her mouth, she came face to face with her irritant, Chris Staller. "What the hell are you doing here?" Katie quizzed.

"I needed to see you, so I got one of the shift nurses to process my paperwork, first thing this morning, before her shift ended. I knew the more time I gave you to think, the worse things would become between us. Can I come in, please?"

What she really wanted to do was knee him in his family jewels for coming here when he should have been resting at the hospital, and for waking her up so damn early. Instead, she stepped away from the doorway and gestured for him to enter her house.

"I can't believe you used that charm of yours like a monopoly game get out of jail free card. You should have at least waited for the doctor to clear you. Then you have the nerve to show up here before seven am. With no coffee in hand, I might add. Are you just looking for trouble?"

"See, you are already avoiding the topic. It's a good thing I came here when I did. Who knows what reaction I would have gotten if I'd waited until tomorrow or Monday? I know it's early, but you said you were planning to go into the office this morning, so I figured I better get right over to charm you some more."

Knowing him, as she did, the look on his face was one of determination so she might as well acquiesce and let him stay.

"Look, you can stay as long as you make some coffee while I go take a quick shower. Something tells me I'm going to need java if you expect me to be cheery and ready to talk. Okay?"

"Whatever you want is what we'll do. I'll get the coffee and wait for you in the kitchen."

"Great, by the way that Band-Aid on your forehead is so much less heart stopping than the mummy gauze from last night."

"Again with the jokes, huh?"

To which Katie simply giggled and walked away with an extra little sway in her hips. How suddenly agreeable he is being, she thought, with a bit of nervous curiosity.as she walked back into her room and to the shower.

It was meant to be a quick wash up, but she found it necessary to shave, just in case. She did not go so far as to put on her makeup, but she did comb her hair and tried to look as presentable as possible. No matter what was about to happen, she wanted to look attractive.

By the time she stepped into the kitchen, Chris was pouring a cup of coffee and setting it next to a plate of pancakes. Katie said nothing, but sat in the chair he had designated for her, and added the necessary items to her coffee. Creamer is what makes it drinkable. Katie was one of those coffee drinkers that really didn't like the taste of the brew.

"I thought you might be hungry and since I woke you from your sleep, I figured I owed you at least some breakfast. I hope you don't mind I used your kitchen."

"I don't mind. Thanks for the pancakes they look great. Can you pass the butter, please?"

They sat in silence for a few minutes each enjoying their respective flapjacks. When Katie was taking her last bite Chris asked if she wanted more and she politely declined. It seemed that was his cue to start his speech.

"Since you don't want to eat any more, I think it's time I explain why I barged in this morning, and then we can talk about it for a while. Sound good?"

"That sounds fine. Do you want to move to the living room? It might be more comfortable."

Chris nodded and after placing both plates in the sink, he followed Katie into the living room. Katie went all the way to one side of the couch and Chris should have known he was supposed to sit at the other, but apparently, he did not want that much distance between them for the talk. Instead, he sat right next to her and made sure that their thighs touched in just the slightest way.

"I was up all night thinking about you and me, and mostly about last night and what it could mean for us. I know that you are resistant to the idea that we can be more than friends. Sometimes it seems that you would rather not even be my friend, to keep it cleaner, safer.

Last night when I woke up in the hospital room and you were there, it was as if the world was right. No one else would have been there for me. I have many people who care about me these days, but no one who makes me complete. I have no one who takes a piece of my heart, my soul, and offers me theirs in return. I wanted so badly to stay still and not wake you, because I was afraid you would leave.

In my heart, I know that we both ended up here so that we could find one another again. In a strange way, I feel like I have been waiting here for you for the last five years. Why do you think I never found a woman to settle down with and start a life? It makes sense to me now why they never seemed to measure up to my ideal. I wasn't going to settle, and I didn't realize until you walked back into my life that I've simply been waiting for you to get here. You are whom I have compared every woman to, and all have failed to measure up to your beauty.

People can see that you are beautiful on the outside, but I see all the other parts of you that make you special. The reason I came here today was to tell you that I love you, I always have, and if you hadn't come back, I would have spent the rest of my life waiting for you and our second chance. You are it for me Katie, and I don't want to lose you again. Please, just give us a shot. Do you think you can do that? Can you love me again?"

Katie didn't say anything at first, but she looked at Chris and saw a tear slide down his cheek. The sight of him was overwhelming. He was all she had been waiting for her entire adult life, and now it was just a matter of being brave enough to take a risk on him, and on love.

"You know, my Dad used to tell me two things that seem to apply to this moment. One was that anything worth having was worth working for and that the effort would make it even sweeter when accomplished.

Secondly, he said that courage was being afraid and doing it anyway. I have been afraid of you since the moment I laid eyes on you again. Even before, really. I was afraid of the way you made me feel. Vulnerable and confused are not two of my favorite emotions. So really, the question is, am I willing to put in the work and do I have the courage to even try?"

Chris kept quiet for once, probably realizing that anything he said could push her in the wrong direction. It took her a moment to say another word. Katie spoke, but it was so soft she doubted Chris heard her at all.

"Did you just say something, because I think you did, but I couldn't hear?" he questioned.

This time looking directly at him, she spoke clearly, "I said yes."

At first, Chris did not respond other than having a goofy look on his face as he stared at her. He looked somewhat dumbfounded, and even though he must have known he was pushing it, he asked for clarification anyway.

"Yes to what?" Men, Katie thought, but she figured she owed him to spell it all out, the man had waited long enough, been persistent long enough, and he deserved this moment.

"Yes to you and me. Yes to giving it a shot. Yes, I have the courage to overcome my fears. Oh and also, yes, I do love you. I don't know that I ever actually stopped loving you, and yes Chris, I want to be with you."

The smile on his face was so broad it made her heart sore to know she had put it there, the man she loved, was finally happy.

"I don't know what to say. I was hoping you would say this and now that you have, I don't have the words to respond. I'm so happy! I can't believe you said yes."

"If you can't tell me, show me," she boldly requested with the look of a young girl who was asking a boy to touch her for the first time. His immediate reaction was a quick intake of breath, and she wasn't sure if it was surprise or desire. Then he looked her in the eyes and she knew it was desire. His hazel eyes burned green.

"Katie, if I touch you please understand that I won't stop at that. My body aches at the thought of you, and I need to make love to you, or not touch you at all." Katie smiled.

"I'm not asking you to just touch me, Chris. I'm asking you to take me to my room, undress me, press your naked body against mine, touch every little bit of my body and make passionate love to me for the rest of the day." He didn't seem to need to hear any more than that. Katie let him take charge from there.

Chris picked her up from the couch and carried her into the bedroom. They kept their eyes locked the whole time as they moved to the room. When Chris laid her down on the bed, he could not believe how lucky he was to be with this woman, a blessing in his life who made every other person seem irrelevant. Chris wanted to make this well worth the wait.

"Lie down and close your eyes. I don't want you to open them until I tell you to. Do you trust me enough to do that, Katie?"

"I trust you Chris or I wouldn't be here right now." She closed her eyes and had no idea what was in store for her.

Chris began the process by removing her boxers and tank top. Lucky for him she was wearing nothing more than those two items, so his work was quick. He asked her to turn over so that her back was to him. This she did without question. Chris used his tongue to lick from between her shoulders down to the small of her back. He blew warm air all the way back up her back and she shuttered just a bit at his breath. Heat against the now cool trail his tongue had left, made her skin super sensitive. It was very erotic to be naked before him, on her bed, with no idea what he was about to do to her. Then he placed his lips on the small of her back and kissed his way around her body.

He nibbled a little at the nape of her neck and licked her skin to make it hot. He expertly applied his tongue to her with utmost care down her back, along her legs, and down to her toes. Chris paid special attention to the little sensitive part of a person's body just behind the knee, along the way. She squirmed every once in a while and made noises that let him know when he found a good spot.

When he finished with her backside he whispered in her ear to turn over, "but keep your eyes closed," and she did just as he asked. She was not used to someone else being in control, but she liked it more than she had ever dreamed she would. Part of her wanted to open her eyes and watch him, as he touched each bit of her body, but the other part was enjoying not knowing where he would touch next.

It was more thrilling than anything she had ever done before, and so simple. His hands made her skin hot and the center of her being was moist and aching for more. Chris stopped caressing her for a moment, but she could feel the intensity of his stare upon her body. In that simple moment, she felt gorgeous and cherished.

"Katie, open your eyes so you can see me." Chris whispered, "I am awestruck by you, the curve of your waist and hips. Your breasts make me ache deep down in a way I didn't even know was possible."

Her response a quiet, "Thank you, please don't stop Chris, I need this."

He moved off the bed and in no time at all, he had removed his clothing. He was the epitome of manhood. His erection so full and substantial, his eyes smoldering in her direction and just the sight of him made her temperature rise. He was gazing at her body and each spot he looked upon felt warmer and tingled. Her breasts were fuller, due to her arousal, and her nipples peaked with the promise of his touch. Chris moved back to the bed, looking down on her with a seductive smile, before he straddled her at the waist. Her skin was hot and she gasped when she felt his hardness against her soft skin.

He blazed a trail of kisses along her stomach, slowly sweeping his tongue between and around her breasts. Katie's back arched, just a little, in an involuntary response when his tongue first hit her skin. By the sound of the groan that escaped through Chris' gritted teeth, she just about broke his will to take it slow. He moved his body down to the edge of the bed, where he started with her legs, and worked his way up to her most cherished spot. This time she squirmed wildly and the noises she made were louder and more frequent, she had not felt this uninhibited ever in her life.

"Chris, you are driving me mad," she said, "Please kiss me. I need to feel your mouth on mine, Chris. Oh God, please, please it feels so good, but I need more. What you must think of me, begging like this."

"I love it! Let go and let me have all of you Katie, I want to make you mine."

"I've only ever been yours, Chris. Take me, I love you"

◆◆◆

Take control he did, he was coachable if nothing else. He rubbed her body, licked her skin, nibbled her softly and then he was between her thighs, kissing her and licking her with his warm, inviting tongue. When she came for him, crying out his name nothing had ever felt as gratifying as satiating the woman he loved. As she whimpered and came down from the high of her orgasm, he was placing gentle kisses around her belly button, and along her tummy.

Chris was impressed with his own ability to stay away from her breasts for so long; it had been beyond difficult for him. They had always been a favorite place of his, but Chris wanted to make her beg for him. He wanted her to admit how badly she wanted him, needed him. He wanted her to admit that her body ached for his touch, his kisses.

To his delight, Katie placed his hands between her breasts and spread them all around for him. It was an enormous turn on, his hands and hers entwined playing with her breasts. Both of them feeling her nipples budded against their palms. For some reason it was the sexiest damn thing he had ever experienced, and he had a feeling it was only the beginning of his awe.

She was this amazing woman and not the girl he remembered any longer, every touch seemed like the most unbelievable thing he had shared with anyone. He was careful not to touch her nipples until she told him he could. They were calling him for sure, but he wanted to wait, he wanted to make her wait.

"Chris, don't be shy," she said as she took his finger and traced her areola. Her back arched the moment his fingers rolled each nipple between his thumb and forefinger. She tried to touch him, but he would not allow it to happen. He used one hand to gently move and then hold both her wrists above her head. She didn't complain and he sensed that she liked it a little.

Finally, when he thought they were both about to explode, he laid his body completely over hers, holding himself up, and using his tongue to entice her and then took each nipple within his mouth. His teeth made Katie groan in sweet, painful ecstasy. He wanted to take her over the edge that he was so masterfully dangling her above.

"Chris, I need you. Oh, please, let me feel you inside me."

He couldn't make her wait forever, nor could he last much longer, his erection was almost unbearable. So, he kissed her thoroughly on the mouth with all the years of pent up passion he felt, while his hand slowly slid down her side to her center. He caressed her and found her to be very wet and ready for him. He had never touched anything so warm; she was by far the most amazing woman he had experienced. She cried out, and Chris thought he might lose it at that exact moment. He forced himself to hold on and be steady. The sounds she made were so earthly and sexy that it drove him mad. He moved his mouth to her breasts and continued to play with her, in an effort to make her yearn for more. He wanted to make her feel better than any man had ever done.

Chris moved his fingers to stroke deep inside her womanhood. She closed her eyes and seemed to enjoy the sensations. She felt so ready and hot for him. He wanted to be inside her, feel the heat of her against his shaft. Chris needed to feel his strength against her most feminine and soft parts. To feel her throb around him, and more than anything, he wanted to take her as his own. He had never felt like such a cave man before. There was this basic need in him to claim him. She cried out his name and he couldn't stand it any longer.

He moved his body above hers and spread Katie's legs with his knee, positioning her perfectly to give her all that she said she wanted, needed, and he hoped more.

"Katie," he said with ragged breath, "look at me Princess."

When she opened her eyes he was slowly entering her and looking into her eyes when he simply said, "I love you." Then he thrust himself into her, filling her up and enjoying the warmth within. The widening of her eyes and the sweet smile on her face told him that she was as close to heaven as he was.

◆ ◆ ◆

She wrapped her legs around him and used her hips to move with him. Neither one of them could look away as the pleasure played across their faces. They were both making the guttural sounds of passion. The more Chris moved within her, the more she needed him. She had enough of not being in control, so she used her legs to maneuver herself and roll him over.

They were separated in the switch, but she enjoyed the look on his face as she mounted him. She slowly slid down until the hot, wet center of her consumed him. She laid her body against his and took his mouth with a bit of force. She wanted to taste him and play with his tongue. She moved slowly up and down him as they kissed.

"No one, but you, has ever made me feel this amazing Princess, no one." He mumbled the words.

Katie could tell by his reaction that he was enjoying the feel of her tongue all over his body. She wanted him to suffer in ecstasy the way he had made her, she wanted him to be at the point of no return, until he needed her fast and hard.

"Katie, my God, you are everything to me. Ride me, now Katie!"

The very idea that she had changed the game and made him beg was a total turn on for her. She was more than ready to take this to the next step. She sat up and leaned back on her heels not letting him leave her body.

"I have been dreaming of this night, after night, since that night you kissed me in my kitchen, and it feels even better than in my dreams. My God, you feel so hard, you fill me up, and I can't wait any longer either."

Katie used his chest to keep her balance and moved her hips back and forth, at first slow, then faster and faster until she thought she might lose her ability to breathe. She could feel the slow vibration start and soon her whole body was tingling. Chris felt her muscles contract around him and knew that her release was coming. Her breathing picked up, as did his. He moaned and she called his name. The tighter her body wrapped around his sex, the more excited he became.

"Oh, Katie, you feel like heaven. Oh baby, come with me, I want to feel you come right now. Please, right now."

She kept up the pace and saw the wave coming in Chris' face. The sight of him, mingled with the feel of him inside her, was too much to handle.

They kept their eyes one other as they called out each other's names in ecstasy. Katie couldn't stop screaming out his name and Chris' voice was so soft that her name sounded like a whisper. She collapsed on his chest and neither one of them said a word until they caught their breaths. Chris was the first to speak.

"That was the most fulfilling experience I have ever had. You are a tomcat. Who knew?"

"You guys will never learn it's always the quiet ones."

They both laughed and just enjoyed lying there together. Their sweat and scents mixed, which had the faint smell of sex, and Katie thought she even smelled the slightest whiff of raspberry.

"You still taste like raspberries," she mentioned with a giggle.

"Thank you, I think? What do you say we take a shower and get un-sweaty?"

"Sounds good to me," Katie replied with a smile, "although I can't imagine what you have against sweaty."

She flashed him the smile of a vixen and licked his nipple before jumping off the bed and running to the bathroom.

They spent the next thirty minutes showering and washing one another free of sex and sweat. Of course bathing each other led to playing with one another and once again, they were taken by their passion for each other.

At one point, she turned and looked over her shoulder at him. She was biting down on her lip out of sheer ecstasy when Chris smiled at her and she thought he never looked more handsome.

"In this moment I am certain that you have never looked sexier. The pleasure you are feeling is written all over your face and for some reason the way you are biting your lip is driving me inane. I am blessed Katie and you are perfection in every way." Chris stated.

"I'm all yours Chris, all of me, now and forever."

That was all it took for him to lose himself, and he thrust into Katie deeper and faster. This time she came first, and the sounds of her pleasure almost drowned out his, as he too went over the edge and found his release.

By the time they were out of her room and in some state of dress, it was after one o'clock in the afternoon. They were both starving, so Katie offered to make some lunch while he picked a good movie for them to watch. When she went into the living room with their food, he was sound asleep on the couch. Katie set their plates down and grabbed a blanket. While she was covering him up, he opened his eyes and moved over on the couch, patting the space he left open for her.

"Lay with me, please. I want to feel your body next to mine while I fall asleep. Remember how good our naps used to be on my Mom's couch?"

She did remember and she couldn't deny him this nap; so she lay next to him, on her couch, and listened as he drifted asleep.

"I love you more than anything, thank you for this chance," he whispered as he drifted to sleep.

"I love you too," was her simple, honest reply.

As she lay there with him, a smile on his face and a steady breath of contentment, she thought about what the last few hours meant for her future. She had taken a huge step and now it would be time to find out if it was courageous or just plain naïve. How was she supposed to know if the words he spoke were true? Could she take the man at his word and forget the boy who hurt her? She desperately wanted to, needed to.

Perhaps she needed to believe in him, even more than he wanted her to. She hoped it was, as she had always dreamed it to be, like a fairy tale – with a happily ever after. Maybe her prince had finally come. She fell asleep dreaming of fairytale weddings, glass slippers, and Chris.

◆◆◆

While she lay dreaming, Chris woke up to feel her body nestled against his, and smiled. Her face looked a little concerned even in sleep. He knew her well enough to know that she had already thought about the consequences of her decision today. It might take a while, but he would prove himself to her. He would prove that things were different now, that she was no longer a naïve young girl, and he was no longer that heartless kid.

This was a new journey, both uncharted and unfamiliar to them. This time they would love one another as love was meant to be, without restriction, without doubt. He had never loved any other woman but Katie. She was the one he was meant to share his life with, the one he had waited for all these years. This time he would not let her slip through his fingers. He would make sure in everything he did that he deserved her love, her trust in him, and then she would stay.

They both knew what the past held for them, and in a way, it was hard for both of them to believe the future could tell a different story. This time it would be the story of a princess, a prince, and beautiful babies all wrapped in a happy home. They wanted the same things; warm nights of cuddling and giggling. It was all within reach, and all very attainable, it just took a little belief on both parts. It was what they had been waiting for all this time, each other.

About the Author

*K*elly Rae lives with her 9-year-old son, Triton, in San Diego, CA. She spends most of her time writing and reading books. She finds inspiration in everyday life, but tries to protect the innocent and occasionally the guilty, in her writing. Chances are you can find her planning a future vacation, with Triton. He says a cruise to the Caribbean, she says maybe Greece! You just never know...

www.facebook.com/kellyraebooks

www.kellyraebooks.com

www.ingramcontent.com/pod-product-compliance
Lightning Source LLC
Chambersburg PA
CBHW050927120626
46552CB00001B/87